Minnesota Vice

Ellen and Mary Kuhfeld

MONICA FERRIS PRESENTS

Minneapolis, Minnesota

January 2017

Copyright 2017, Ellen and Mary Kuhfeld

ISBN-13: **978-1-877934-11-7**

DEDICATION

Sincere thanks to

The Aaardvarks Writers' Group

Cathleen Jordan

And the Twin Sisters in Crime

CONTENTS

ACKNOWLEDGMENTS

Ellen and Mary Kuhfeld

"An Ill Wind" originally published in *Alfred Hitchcock's Mystery Magazine*, (*AHMM*) April 1984

"Allergic to Death", *AHMM* September 1984

"The Scales of Justice", *AHMM* December 1985

"Night Light", *AHMM* March 1987

"Timely Psychiatric Intervention", *AHMM* September 1986

"A Specialist in Dragons", *AHMM* May 1987

Ellen Kuhfeld

"The Old Shell Game", *AHMM* January 1986

"Thorolf and the Peacock", *AHMM* June 1987

"Dances With Werewolves", *Tales of the Unanticipated*, Autumn 2006

"Cycles of Violence", *Beyond Centauri* October 2008

Cover images

© Can Stock Photo Inc. / HelleM

© Can Stock Photo Inc. / Tisskananat

AN ILL WIND

It wasn't fair. Yesterday afternoon Hedeby had broken all records for late December by about ten degrees. Shirtsleeve kids had thrown frisbees to leaping dogs. Old folks had puttered in their yards. It had peaked at three with sixty-four warm, sunny degrees. Of course, by seven it had clouded up and by nine it had started to rain. By midnight last night, when he came on duty, it was sleeting. And this morning, under a bitter, driving wind, there were sixteen inches of snow on the ground. With more still coming. It wasn't fair. His shift would be over in fifteen minutes, but the streets were blocked; he couldn't get home. Which was just as well; his relief wouldn't be able to get in. Hafner went to the second-story window and scraped a little circle in the frost. The snow was flying horizontally down Broad Street. Technically the sun was up, but all it could do was turn the buildings across the street into gray silhouettes against a gray sky. Jesus, a real Minnesota blizzard.

Doggedly trying to see the good in the situation, Hafner reflected that it would probably be a quiet shift. Even the most ambitious criminal would hole up in weather like this.

He heard someone coming down the hall and, surprised, reached for his suit coat. He only had one arm in its sleeve when the squad room door opened, and he froze in astonishment at the apparition before him.

It was tall, way over six feet; bulky, and encased in snow and ice. Its face was a glitter of tiny icicles spangled over a blue ski mask. And topping that, also covered by ice and snow, was a plastic fire helmet several sizes too small. A tiny red light atop the helmet flashed bravely through the ice and a toy siren was sounding.

The figure reached up, shedding slabs of snow, and removed the helmet. "Like it?"

Hafner recognized the voice. "Nygaard! You bastard, you like to scared me to death! What are you doing here?"

"I work here, remember? It's time for me to go on duty." Nygaard pulled off the ski mask, revealing a blocky red face under a sheaf of straight blond hair. He walked stiffly into the room.

Hafner, a smaller, darker man, by nature neat and conservative, got out of his way. "Hold it, dammit! You're shedding all over everything! Why didn't you take that snowsuit off out in the hall?"

"Well, hell, Jack, it's dark out in the hall; I couldn't find the zippers!" Because of the blizzard, the police department was mostly unmanned, and almost all of the lights were turned off. Nygaard bent to dig for the zipper in the left leg of his suit, flinging bits of melting snow in all directions.

"Watch where you're throwing that stuff, for Christ's sake! Anyway, how'd you get here? I heard all the roads are closed."

"They are. But I bought a snowmobile last year, and it just eats up weather like this." Nygaard began picking at the zipper of his other leg with massive fingers. "The department ought to buy a couple of them. Issue blue ski masks — red for the plainclothes," he said, with a broad grin. He unzipped the leg to the knee then straightened and began the same operation on his sleeves. "I had no problem at all coming in. You got to watch out for the buried fireplugs, though; they can tear the bottom out of your machine."

"You're crazy, you know that?"

"So they tell me," replied Nygaard indifferently, unseaming the suit from chin to crotch and stepping out of it. Underneath, he was wearing jeans and a blue plaid flannel shirt. He was almost as massive a presence out of the suit as in it. He took the suit out into the hall to beat most of the snow and ice off it, then came back to hang it on the coat rack. He looked around at the empty desks. "So," he said, "I guess we're it for detectives, huh? Anything going down?" He sat on the edge of his desk, shifting his belt holster so his gun wouldn't poke him in the kidney.

"Are you kidding? In this weather? And a good thing, too; I'm not dressed to go out in this." Hafner took his suit coat back off and hung it carefully over the back of a chair. It belonged to his best suit, a lightweight wool blend in a black pinstripe. He'd been scheduled for a court appearance today, after he got off duty, and so had dressed up. "I've got no gloves, no hat and no boots," he complained. "The frickin' weatherman said cloudy, with showers, so I just wore my raincoat in last night."

"Yeah, I heard him," said Nygaard, grinning. "How about we call him up and tell him he oughta help us shovel the eighteen inches of cloudy off our sidewalk?"

Despite himself, Hafner chuckled. Thor Nygaard was bright, inventive and cheerful: at twenty-seven their youngest detective, and the screwiest man alive.

"Anyone else here?"

"Some of the night shift left over. There's four uniforms, one on the front desk, one running the switchboard, one upstairs helping Deputy Marsh hold down the jail, and one trying to rustle up enough grounds to make us some coffee."

"Oh, God, no coffee?" groaned Nygaard. He could drink a gallon of coffee per shift.

"There's about a cup left."

Nygaard went to lift his mug off one of the hooks beside the twenty-cup maker. "Maybe a store will open up later and I can take the snowmobile on a food run."

Hafner brightened. "Yeah, Ferguson over on Humphrey lives upstairs from his grocery store. Maybe he'll open up. Good idea. Otherwise it's cheese curls and Hershey bars from the machine."

Nygaard tipped the coffee maker to drain the bitter dregs into his mug, which was light blue and said *uff da* − Norwegian for *oy vey* − in yellow. Hafner asked, "What was the idea of that crazy helmet you were wearing when you came in?"

"Visibility is almost zero, out there. I was wishing out loud I had a light and siren for the snowmobile when Eric handed me his favorite toy. He was so pleased to be helpful, how could I tell him no?" The big cop looked fondly at his son's helmet, which was stealthily wetting down the master copy of a monthly arrest report. He tasted his coffee and made a face, but resolutely drank more.

The snow began to let up an hour later, and by ten the sky was clearing. Patrolman Davis had borrowed some coffee from the jail and the red light on the twenty-cup maker was glowing comfortingly. Hafner sat near the window nursing a cup − his mug was white and said nothing − and watched as the sun came shyly out. The street outside was a lushly draped and sparkling desert. Drifts came halfway up doors, and blue hollows had formed around lampposts and the back of an abandoned car.

Most of Hedeby's city employees were themselves snowed in; so despite the clear skies, all but the main arteries were going to stay blocked for hours. Hafner watched a big snowplow struggle to clear a single lane up Broad Street, walling in the abandoned car in the process.

Nygaard's phone rang, and he scooped up the receiver with a big hand. "Detective Division, Sergeant Nygaard, may I help you?"

Hafner could hear the gabble of an excited voice from his place by the window. He stiffened and listened alertly to Nygaard's end of the conversation.

"Yes, all right; now calm down. What's your name?" Nygaard grabbed a pencil and began to scrawl. "Where are you right now? No, I mean the address. And that's where the body is? Who is the deceased? You're absolutely sure she's dead? I see, yeah, yeah. Now look, you stay there, but don't touch anything. That's very important. No, we'll be out. Yes, I'm aware the streets are blocked, but we'll get there."

Nygaard threw the receiver back into its cradle and said, "It's Sarah Fiske. Dead, apparently murdered by a burglar."

"Jesus Christ!" Hafner jumped to his feet. Old Mrs. Fiske was the town's most famous eccentric: reclusive, crotchety, very well-off. "Who found her?"

"George Grimby." Nygaard looked at his notes. "He says he came and cleared her sidewalks, then didn't get an answer when he knocked to get paid. He went around to the back, found the back door unlocked, and the place ransacked. She was in the living room, her head beaten in."

"Is he the Grimby with a poker game in his basement every Wednesday night?"

"Sounded like him." George Grimby's two sources of income were a weekly poker game and a string of odd jobs he did around town. He was "known to the police," but since a number of important people – including the police chief – turned up on occasion at the poker games, they hadn't been raided in several years.

"He there now?"

"Yeah. Have you ever ridden on a snowmobile?"

"No, why?"

"Because we've got to go take a look, that's why. And the snowmobile is the only way we've got of getting there. Grab the kit. I'll go look in the property room for something warm you can wear."

Hafner soon found himself in a too-big overcoat, patched wellington boots, and a large hat made of gray bunny fur. He drew the line at the white mittens with yellow daisies embroidered on them; instead he stuck his hands into the pockets of Nygaard's snowmobile suit and suffered the wind to blow up the sleeves of his borrowed overcoat.

But worst of all, Nygaard insisted on wearing that goddam siren helmet. It was only a fifteen minute ride to Mrs. Fiske's house, but there were people out shoveling their walks, glad for an excuse to stop and stare. Hafner buried his face in Nygaard's broad back and hoped the big coat and furry hat were disguise enough.

7

Mrs. Fiske's house was on a big, tree-studded corner lot. It was a Spanish colonial with a red tile roof and wrought-iron trim at the windows. An orange snowblower stood, snow-clogged, by the front steps.

The door opened as they walked up; apparently George Grimby had been looking out the window for them.

"Thank God, thank God," he exclaimed. "Come in!" He gave a startled glance at the toy helmet, but apparently found nothing strange about the fur hat. He was a small, slat-thin man with shifty eyes and bad teeth. He wore a ragged blue jacket over two pairs of overalls.

The two detectives stomped snow off their boots in the entrance hall and peered into the living room. Nygaard made a sucking noise through his teeth. It was a very thoroughly ransacked room: In addition to the usual burglary-type disorder, the couch was overturned, the heavy drapes were in a tumble on the floor and the carpet was pulled up along one wall.

"She tried to fight him off, you think?" asked Hafner.

"Dunno," said Nygaard doubtfully.

Near the brick fireplace lay the body of a woman in her sixties. She had an aristocratic nose and what had once been a carefully arranged bun of graying hair. She was wearing a dark silk dress. A fireplace poker lay near the body.

Hafner unbuttoned the borrowed topcoat as he walked into the living room, but didn't take it off; it was cold in the house. He glanced around, absorbing detail, then knelt beside the body, putting a heavy metal case down within reach. "Have you touched her?" he asked.

Grimby said nervously, "I touched her hand, but it was cold and − and kind of stiff, so I knew she was dead. That's why I called you instead of an ambulance."

Hafner pried open an eye and found her glaring in an affronted way at him through a clouded cornea, so he closed it again.

"How did you happen to find her?" he asked.

"Well, like I told you guys when I called, I came to plow the city sidewalk and the walk up to her front door. I do stuff like that for her — yard work and such. We have — had an agreement that every time it snowed I'd do her walks. She always paid on the spot, cash, so I came up to get my money and she didn't answer the door." He looked around at the drawn blinds and shrugged. "She's almost always home, y'know. Sends out for anything she needs. I came around to the back, saw the back door open a little. That surprised me; she keeps her doors closed and locked all the time. So I looked in. The kitchen was a wreck, and she didn't answer when I called out, so I came in to see if she was all right, and here she was." His little dark eyes darted from one to the other, as if to see if they believed him. He must not have liked what he saw, because he said, "Now hold on! You can see she's been dead awhile, can't you? All cold and stiff? So it wasn't me! I just got here!"

Nygaard said, "I'll go look around, all right?"

"Go ahead," Hafner said.

Grimby said, "I got some other snow clearing to do. Can I go now?"

Hafner said, too politely, "May I ask you to stay awhile? There may be more questions I or my partner will want to ask you, if you don't mind, Mr. Grimby."

Again the nervous shifting of the eyes. "Sure. Always willing to cooperate, that's me." He went to stand near the overturned couch, and tried not to look too curious about Hafner's examination of the late Mrs. Fiske.

There were two distinct places where she had been struck on the head: once on the crown and again just into the hairline behind her temple. There may have been more skull injuries, but he couldn't see without moving her, and he didn't want to disturb the body until it had been photographed. Both blows had broken her skull, and either of them might have proven fatal. There was no other visible evidence of injury. Grimby had been right about the stiff hand; rigor was well established in the body.

Hafner opened the kit and got out a little brush and a jar of gray powder. "You live, what, five-six blocks from here, Mr. Grimby?"

"Uh, yes."

He dusted the handle of the poker, but it had been wiped clean. That was to be expected; everyone knew about fingerprints nowadays. "How did you get here through all the snow?"

"Used the snowblower. I had two other jobs on my way, so I did them, and just cleared a little path the rest of the way."

"Did you notice any footprints around the house when you came?"

Grimby thought and shook his head. "No. No, I'm sure I didn't."

"When did you see her last?"

"Yesterday."

"Really? What time yesterday?"

Grimby drew his shoulders up as the possible meaning of that 'really' sank in. "'Bout ten, I think. Before noon, anyhow."

"You saw her here, at home?"

". . . Yeah. She got this idea she wanted to see tulips over her breakfast table next spring, so she called me up and asked me to come over. She told me to dig up the tulips I planted in her front yard in October and put them under her kitchen window. I come over to spade up a flower bed. Took me two hours, and she paid me ten dollars."

"Was she wearing the dress she has on now?"

Grimby glanced at the body and away again. "No, somethin' a lighter color, with flowers, I think."

"Was she here alone?"

Grimby shrugged. "I guess so. I didn't see nobody else. But I wasn't really lookin', y'know. I didn't come in, 'cause I was all over dirt. She paid me at the back door and I left."

"I see. Is there a relative of hers in town you know of, Mr. Grimby? We need someone to make formal identification and tell us where the body is to go."

"Just one, a nephew. Lives right up the street. Whenever she didn't like my work she'd threaten to get him to do it. But she never did."

"What's his name?"

"Mr. Olson. I don't know his front name."

Nygaard came back into the living room while Hafner was sighing his way down the long list of Olsons in the phone book — Hedeby was heavily Scandinavian — looking for the Olson who lived a few numbers up on Seventh Street. Hafner stopped looking long enough to ask, "Find anything?"

"The whole house looks as bad as this room. Who are you going to call?"

"Ah, here it is. A Mr. Randolph Olson. He's her nephew. I'll ask him to come over."

"Fine. It's cold in here because the thermostat is turned down low and there's a broken window in the kitchen."

Hafner was dialing, using the back of his pen and holding the receiver in a peculiar way so as not to disturb any fingerprints. "That the means of entry?"

"Come see for yourself."

Randolph Olson agreed, after expressions of shock, to come over. He proved to be a tall, bluff, hearty man with a red face and a meager cover of dark hair. He shied visibly at the sight of his aunt. "Oh, my," he said. "Poor old thing!"

"I take it she is Sarah Fiske?" asked Hafner.

"Oh, yes. Er, couldn't you cover her or something? She looks indecent."

She didn't look indecent to Hafner. She looked like a formidable dowager who was about to sit up and order everyone out. "I wish we could cover her, Mr. Olson," said Hafner. "But we didn't bring anything with us, and we don't want to use anything in the house until the investigation is complete."

"If she makes you uncomfortable, come out into the kitchen," said Nygaard. "In fact, everyone come. I've got some questions, if you don't mind."

"Sure," said Olson.

"All right," said Grimby.

The kitchen was high-ceilinged, like the rest of the downstairs. It was very large and well equipped, if old fashioned. A number of the cabinets had been emptied onto the tile floor, and the men stepped carefully. "Please be careful," warned Nygaard when Olson started to approach the broken window.

"Eh?" said Olson, stopping. "This is where he got in, right? The burglar."

"Looks like it," said Nygaard. "So please don't step in the glass under the window. We can learn things from it."

Olson stared at the shards on the floor, some of which had fallen on scattered tea leaves. "You can? What sorts of things?"

"Oh, whether it was cut out or smashed. Things like that."

"I see."

"I never seen a burglarized house before," said Grimby. "I didn't know they left such a mess."

"There are some unusual features to this burglary," said Nygaard. "For example, here in the kitchen he cleaned out some of the shelves entirely and left others completely alone. I wonder if he wasn't more out to make a mess than to look for valuables."

"How do you mean?" asked Olson sharply.

"Well, that high shelf, for example," said Nygaard. He walked carefully to one of the cupboards and gestured up at a shelf. "See, the one with the sugar bowl on it, and the big platters. It hasn't been touched, but a sugar bowl is traditionally the place where householders keep money." Nygaard reached up and stuck a forefinger into the bowl, drawing it out coated whitely. He was easily tall enough to do so without otherwise disturbing the bowl. He grinned and sucked the finger clean. "Nope, just sugar."

"Maybe he was too short to reach up that high," said Hafner.

"No, on the contrary, I think he was a tall man," said Nygaard.

"Well, since I'm only five-six, can I go?" asked Grimby.

"No, sir, not just yet," said Hafner, who had gone to squat over the broken window pane.

"Mr. Olson, when did you last see your aunt?" asked Nygaard.

"Yesterday. She invited me to dinner." He looked around the kitchen, saw the open refrigerator door. "See, there's the leftover pot roast. She had time to clear away and wash up before the burglar came."

"Dumb burglar, to come in while she was still up," said Hafner.

"How do you know that?" asked Grimby.

"She's fully dressed. No one dresses to come down and confront a burglar," said Hafner.

"Maybe it happened this morning," suggested Olson. "She's a very early riser."

"Can you imagine a burglar out blundering around in that storm?" said Hafner aggrievedly.

"Did you have lunch regularly with your aunt?" asked Nygaard.

"Oh, perhaps twice a month. To discuss her investments. I like to think I have a certain understanding of the stock market."

"Was she a wealthy woman?" asked Hafner.

Olson became judicious. "That depends on your definition of wealth. Not a millionaire, certainly. But comfortable, very comfortable."

"Are you a stockbroker?" asked Nygaard.

"No, no, nothing like that. I was left a small inheritance some years back, and I live on that. I dabble, merely dabble, with investments."

"Does Mrs. Fiske have any children?" asked Hafner.

"No. The family has not been very − er, prolific, in recent generations. I myself am a bachelor, and, in fact, my aunt's only living relative, apart from a cousin and his family in Des Moines. He has four children by three wives, a remarkable record when one considers how much of his life has been spent behind bars." Olson touched the hair above one ear in a gratified way. "Phillip has been quite a disappointment to Aunt Sarah."

"Mr. Grimby says your aunt stayed at home most of the time. Is that correct?" asked Hafner.

"Yes, she didn't like − er, rubbing elbows with strangers," said Olson. "And she never went anywhere after Thanksgiving; she claimed that was the reason she never had a cold." He shrugged, somewhat embarrassed. "She was a trifle eccentric, you know. But a lovely lady, lovely. And very generous to me."

"Generous?" asked Nygaard.

"Her needs were modest, so she supplemented my income with a monthly allowance. I reciprocated with financial advice. For instance, I had advised her that it was possible to divest herself of some of her wealth at some future date to avoid death duties. That was the subject of our dinner meeting. I offered to handle the matter for her."

"This 'divestment' − was any of it to come to you?" asked Nygaard.

"Here, now, I find that question impertinent," said Olson stiffly. But Nygaard only waited, so he went on, "Well, yes, a great deal of it was to be mine. But you seem to forget, sir: If she was going to give it to me, I had no motive to kill her."

"Now, no one's making any accusations just yet," said Hafner. "We're here to collect facts and hold things down until a proper investigative team arrives, okay?"

"Sorry, you'll have to excuse me; I'm upset," apologized Olson. "This is a shocking thing, shocking. My poor aunt — " He tried to repress a sob, or effect one, Hafner couldn't tell which.

"Yes, the killer was a cold-blooded bastard," said Nygaard.

"What makes you say that?" asked Grimby.

"He couldn't have ransacked the house with her standing there watching. And, by both your and Mr. Olson's statements, she didn't come in from outside and surprise him. So he killed her and then spent a long time searching the house. Most burglars panic and bolt if they happen to kill someone."

"Why — why, that's very clever of you," said Olson.

Hafner asked, "Was your aunt in the habit of keeping cash and valuables in the house?"

"Unfortunately, yes," replied Olson. "Her father lost half his fortune when two of the banks in town failed back in the thirties, so she kept only a minimum balance in a single savings account. Whenever a dividend or interest check arrived, she would go cash it. There may have been several thousand in cash in this house. A nasty habit, and a stupid one, but there you are. And she had a lot of fine silver and some good pieces of jewelry."

Grimby glanced into the big pantry. "Looks like he found the silver," he said, nodding at an empty wooden chest laying open on the shelf. A drift of flour across its green felt lining echoed conditions outside.

Hafner went to the broken window, careful not to disturb the broken glass, and peered out. An icy wind made him pull the too-big overcoat closed. "What's in the garage?" he asked. It was a two-car garage, with an enormous drift leaning up against the door.

"A '49 Cadillac, almost a collector's item, I guess," said Olson. "I doubt if it has ten thousand miles on it."

"It's up on blocks," offered Grimby. "I did that for her the day after Thanksgiving, the same day I put her lawn furniture in there."

"How about we go take a look?" said Nygaard.

Hafner started to object, then caught the meaning look on Nygaard's face. "All right," he said. "You two both stay here, okay?"

"Can we turn the heat up?" asked Grimby — the snow on his overalls was melting and he was shivering.

"'Fraid not," said Hafner. "I want everything left just as it is. Each of you watch the other to make sure nothing is accidentally moved, okay?"

Grimby and Olson looked at each other warily. "Sure," said Grimby, and Olson nodded affirmatively.

The two policemen waded through the snow to the garage. Inside, one half was taken up with the large and elderly Cadillac, the other filled with lawn care equipment and lawn furniture. Like the car, everything was old but of good quality and in excellent repair. Nothing had been disturbed, which did not seem to surprise them.

"What do you think?" asked Hafner.

"Did you see those tea leaves all over the floor? Apparently Mrs. Fiske liked to make her tea without bags."

"So?"

"There are pieces of broken glass from the window laying on top of some of them."

"Yeah, I saw that," said Hafner. He stuffed his hands in his pockets and wished Nygaard had suggested they go up to one of the bedrooms in the house. "Grimby said he dug a flower bed yesterday under her kitchen windows and planted tulip bulbs for her. Are you thinking we'll find only Grimby's footprints in it?"

"We'd find no one's," said Nygaard, pulling his ski mask down over his ears. He had rolled it up so it resembled a knit cap. "Grimby would've raked his out when he finished digging it up. And no one's been across it since. That window was broken after the kitchen was trashed — cut out, then dropped on the floor to make it look like it was done from the outside. There's a glass cutter in one of the kitchen drawers. She was killed by someone she'd let into the house."

"So you think Grimby, too. I agree, no real burglar searched that house. Tearing up the carpet, for Christ's sake — ! Grimby knew about the money, and he could have come back in the evening, after Olson left. And he's not exactly a law-abiding citizen."

"No, not Grimby," disagreed Nygaard. "Come on, can't you see what happened?" The big detective touched the side of his nose and said, "Olson comes to dinner and Aunt Sarah tells him she's going to stop helping him out. Or maybe that she's changing her will, leaving all the money to a home for retired cat-fanciers or something. Because consider that jerk. Even dead, did Mrs. Fiske look like the kind of sweet dumb old lady who'd take fiscal advice from someone like Olson?"

"Well . . . " said Hafner. Because he personally wouldn't trust Olson to make change for a dollar.

"It might be interesting to check on the way his own investments have been doing lately. I bet he's got a real case of the shorts. Did you see his shoes? Expensive, but badly-worn. Same for those trousers. No, he's our man, all right. So he comes to dinner and hears the bad news. He follows her into the living room, trying to talk her out of it. But she's a stubborn old lady. So he grabs the poker and lets her have it."

"There's a blow on the top of her head, near the back, consistent with a blow from behind. And another that might have been struck after she fell," Hafner said.

"From behind? She wouldn't turn her back on a stranger," said Nygaard. "Right?"

"She'd turn her back on Grimby."

Nygaard ignored that. "So there he is with a body. What to do? Aha, make it look like it happened after he left. She's a recluse, right? Hardly ever a visitor. In a day or so it will be impossible to tell just when it happened. So he cleans up in the kitchen, washing dishes and putting things away. Then he tries to make it look as if a very thorough burglar's paid a call. But he's never seen a burglarized house, and he overdoes it. And he breaks the window in the kitchen only after he's finished pulling things out, after he's spilled her tea leaves on the floor. It's dark out by then; he doesn't see the new flowerbed, so he doesn't think about footprints."

"How do you know there aren't footprints under all that snow?" argued Hafner. "Grimby's footprints."

"Naw, Grimby's smarter than that. He'd have chosen a different window."

"Or put on outsize boots, and left fake footprints," said Hafner. "He didn't know it was going to snow, remember. Suppose there are footprints? Dammit, Grimby's a crook!"

"Is he? Our beloved chief plays poker with him about once a month, and so do Mayor Anderson and Judge Lundquist. The game may not be legal, but I bet it's honest."

Hafner, unconvinced, shrugged, blew on his cold hands, and turned to look around.

There was one shiny new object in the garage, a strange contraption that looked like a cross between a vacuum cleaner and an outboard motor, with buckles and straps. Hafner stared at it. Catching Nygaard's grin at his mystification, he growled, "All right, wise guy: What is it?"

"A leaf blower. You buckle it on and it blows your leaves into a big pile − or into your neighbor's yard, if you're out of plastic bags. A friend of mine has one, and I borrowed it once. It's like wearing a jet plane, but it works real well. You really think Grimby?"

"Oh, hell, yeah. Stands out all over him. Twitchy, nervous, couldn't look me in the eye."

"He's always like that."

"How do you know?"

"Same way I know how often hizzoner sits in the poker game. Tell me, when did Grimby do it? What did you find when you looked at the body?"

"She's been dead at least twelve hours. Rigor's completely established, which takes eight to twelve hours, coming on quicker if it's colder — and it's cold in the house. But her corneas are clouded, which takes between twelve and twenty-four hours if the eyes are closed, and they were." Hafner had consulted a Crossly Checklist taped to the inside lid of the investigations kit to determine the time of death.

Nygaard looked at his watch. "Twelve hours ago would make it eleven last night. If she's a very early riser, she'd've been in bed before then. Say she was dead by ten at the latest. If they lingered over coffee, Olson might not have gotten out of there until eight. That's cutting it fine, if Grimby came after Olson left."

"If he left at eight, that's two hours."

"An autopsy will show how soon after her meal she died. I'm betting it was immediately."

"And I'm thinking it wasn't. So what do you suggest, we arrest both of them? I don't think we have enough evidence to hold either of them, if it comes down to it. Damn, I wish we could get a look at that flowerbed! But we'd spoil the evidence if we used a shovel, and I'm hanged if I'm going to get out there on my hands and knees with a camelhair brush. It'll be hours before we can get a crew out here."

"We'll have to let them go — and the guilty one will pack his bags and rabbit." It was Nygaard's turn to look dispiritedly around the big garage. "You know, if I had one of those leaf blowers and a pair of skis, I wouldn't need my snowmobile. I wonder — Here, gimme a hand!" He went to lift the device off the wall.

"The crazy helmet wasn't enough for you?" asked Hafner incredulously.

"No, I'm serious! C'mon, this thing's heavy!"

Reluctantly, Hafner went to help Nygaard fasten the contraption on his back. The metal was cold enough to make him hiss when his bare hands touched it. But when Nygaard explained his idea, he nodded, then went gratefully back into the house, where it was a little warmer.

"What's he doing out there?" demanded Olson a few minutes later, bending to look out the broken window as Nygaard approached from outside.

"That's Mrs. Fiske's leaf blower!" said Grimby. "Hey, he's started it up!"

The trio watched in amazement as the big man vanished behind a cloud of snow.

"He's uncovering a flower bed," said Hafner.

"There's no flower bed under this window," said Olson.

"Yes, there is," said Grimby. "I dug it up myself just yesterday. I know what he's doing; he's looking for footprints, right? The burglar's footprints."

"Yes, that's right," said Hafner. "It would have been impossible for anyone to have climbed through that window without leaving footprints. Unless, of course, he didn't climb through the window at all, but broke it after Mrs. Fiske let him in, after he killed her and tore the house apart to make it look like a burglar was here."

Grimby made a whistling mouth, but no sound came out. Olson, on the other hand, made a dash for the front door. Hafner, startled, let him get halfway to the door before running after him. By the time he caught up with him, Olson was sitting on the snowmobile, trying to find the starter.

Hafner dragged him off the machine and threw him face down into a snowdrift, and sat on him while fumbling his handcuffs out. Snow shovelers stopped to stare. Hafner said, "Randolph Olson, you are under arrest. You have the right to remain silent – "

"I want a lawyer!" yelled Olson.

"You have the right to consult with an attorney," agreed Hafner, hauling Olson's right hand up and fastening it to his left. "If you want an attorney and can't afford one, we'll provide one for you."

"I'm not that broke," muttered Olson, a damaging admission. Hafner took him back inside.

"All right, how did you know?" asked Hafner, after Nygaard had put the leaf blower away and come into the house.

"Grimby's too short."

"Too short to what? Climb in through that window?"

"No, too short to put that sugar bowl way up there. And why would he? He isn't the one trying to make it look like Mrs. Fiske cleared up the dinner things after he left. She certainly didn't put it way up there. The only other things up on that shelf were things she never used, like those platters, for the sort of big dinners she didn't throw any more. What was a sugar bowl full of sugar – meaning she used it every day – doing up there? Olson's a bachelor; he's never been taught not to put things you use every day up on the high shelves where the women can't get at them."

Hafner thought that over. It was simple once you saw it, just like his answer to the problem of clearing the snow away. He grinned. "Can I ask you to come along with me on my next case?" he asked in honest admiration.

Nygaard grinned back. "Sure."

"After the snow melts, of course. So we can drive a car."

Hafner agreed to stay at the house to direct a more thorough investigation when the crew arrived. And Mr. Olson suffered the indignity of having his hands cuffed around Sergeant Nygaard's substantial waist for a snowmobile ride downtown – to the accompaniment of a child's toy siren and flashing red light.

ALLERGIC TO DEATH

It had been a long, cold, lingering winter; but now the season had turned, the air waxed warm, and the bees and flowers were doing a prodigious trade in nectar and pollen. Parks and yards were ablaze with tulips, elms dripped catkins on the sidewalk, and even vacant lots were golden with dandelions.

Jack Hafner and Thor Nygaard were supposed to have the afternoon off. Hafner was scheduled for his annual physical; Nygaard was going to take his son fishing. But there they were in the squad room on the second floor of Hedeby's police department, listening to a determined old woman insisting there'd been a murder. Impatiently, they heard her out.

Four days ago, she said, her brother-in-law had been found dead by his housekeeper. Ralph Bjornlund had just turned 82, and was the wealthy member of his family, better off than any of the others. "And he was a mean, crotchety old thing, too," she said. "So there was no feeling of kindness or gratitude to hold his killer's hand. Why, there was many a time I felt like smacking him myself."

Hafner nodded agreement; the police were very familiar with Ralph Bjornlund. They had fielded a constant stream of complaints from the old man about his neighbors and their children, who were all thieves, noisemakers, trespassers and vandals to hear him tell it. And they had to handle him carefully: the man was not only wealthy and influential, but had a weak heart and severe asthma. It would not have done to infuriate him that one straw more, and trigger an attack.

"What makes you think his death was suspicious?" asked Hafner.

Helga Bjornlund, a little old lady with angry-pink cheeks and an outraged look in her pale blue eyes, replied: "They said he must have gone for a walk in his back yard, and had an asthma attack. Nonsense! Ralph knew better than to go out in a yard full of pollen, any more than he'd eat eggs for breakfast or allow a cat in his house. If he wanted to take a walk, he chose rainy days, or wore a mask.

"The medical examiner came and looked at the body; and when I asked, he said, 'No, Ralph didn't have his inhaler in his pocket.' He would have gone out into that dry, sunny yard without his inhaler only at gunpoint. And make no mistake, he knew how bad the pollen was out there."

"How's that?" asked Nygaard.

"He had a pollen counter by his window," said Mrs. Bjornlund. "I've seen him consult it, then call the radio station to confirm the count. He was very careful. I wish I had stayed in town, but I absolutely had to go; it was the state florists' convention, and I was to give a talk on the problems and benefits of a one-person operation. The medical examiner said he wanted to perform an autopsy. I said nothing; I assumed he would, and I was waiting to see what the results were. You see, it may not have been pollen at all, but poison.

"Then I got home — and there was nothing but an urn of ashes. No autopsy at all. So here I am. And I tell you, he was murdered! Now that he's been cremated, his body can't be tested. But you're the police, and I'm sure you have other ways of finding out. I want something done!"

More to get rid of her than for any other reason, the pair promised to look into it. The lady went away, Hafner's physical confirmed his suspicion he was in excellent health, and Nygaard's boy fell out of the boat into Lake Birka.

Thor was still laughing over it the next morning. "I hauled him out by the scruff of his neck," he said to Hafner, "and be damned if he didn't still have hold of his rod — and be double damned if the sunfish wasn't still on the line!" Nygaard was a very big man, with a thick sheaf of straight blond hair and a lot of jaw. His laugh was a loud haw, haw, haw, an infectious noise.

"You'd better have it mounted", Jack said, smiling. "Fish stories work better when you can point at the fish. You'll be telling this one for quite a while, and your son after you. That fish could become an heirloom."

Thor went to refill his blue mug with black coffee and came back more serious. "Gonna be rough investigating a possible murder when the body's been cremated."

"If Helga Bjornlund thought something was funny, why didn't she hang around to make sure they autopsied him?" Jack said aggrievedly.

"She's inherited the biggest share of his estate, you know," said Nygaard. "I already called City Hall to ask about the will."

"Is that so?" said Hafner, his dark eyes glinting. "Well, how about that? Any other relatives?"

"A brother and a niece."

"So maybe she's scared one of them will say something, and decided to raise the question herself."

"Or, maybe she's right; one of them killed him," said Nygaard. "Or someone outside the family."

Hafner nodded. "Or maybe the doctor was right, and he died of natural causes."

Thor laughed. "Now that we've covered all the possibilities, who gets to phone Dr. Stark?"

"You do it. I've got a burglary report to wind up."

Christian Stark, the Medical Examiner, greeted Nygaard familiarly. "Something I can do for you?" he asked.

"Remember old Ralph Bjornlund? Died about a week ago?"

"Yeah, heart attack. Why?"

"Someone came in yesterday to say she thought he'd been murdered."

Dr. Stark snorted. "Baloney! Poor old guy, he was allergic to just about everything in the world, had been for years. Had asthma, too. It's a wonder he lasted as long as he did."

"You were the one who went to see him when the report came in?"

"Yes. Looked like he went out for a walk, had an asthma attack which triggered his heart. That was the first time I'd seen him professionally; he went to a specialist in Minneapolis. When they put his house up for sale, I'll be tempted to put in a bid."

Surprised, Nygaard asked, "What for? He lived in a house the size of City Hall. All your kids have left home now, haven't they?"

Dr. Stark said, "Yes. But it's got an air conditioning system you wouldn't believe. The place is almost hermetically sealed, and the air that does get in is filtered, cooled or heated, has moisture added or taken out – it's like a perfect day in the mountains, being in that house. And I've got a few allergies myself, including hay fever. Spring and fall are hell on people like me."

"So why did he go outdoors for a walk?"

"Beats me. He might not have realized how bad the air was outside, how full of pollen it was. Like I said, inside his house, it was sheer heaven."

"New system, huh? He wasn't used to how well it worked?"

Dr. Stark hesitated. "Well, no. I guess he'd had it for a couple of years, anyway."

"Our informant thought you were going to do an autopsy, but didn't. How come?"

"His brother objected. And there was nothing to justify one, really. He was an old man with a bad heart, asthma and a lot of allergies. His back yard had several big trees and was full of flowers, including a big lilac bush right by the door. I had to stop once during my examination to use my inhaler."

"Found him outdoors, then?"

"No, he managed to stagger back inside. He was right inside the back door."

"If he was so allergic, why did he have a yard full of flowers?"

"Same reason I do," explained Dr. Stark patiently. "He liked to stand inside his air conditioned house and look out at them. They're very pretty."

"Did Helga Bjornlund also object to an autopsy?"

"Helga — she's the little white-haired one? His brother's widow?"

"Yes."

"No, not to me. I explained to the brother that I didn't consider anything suspicious, but it would help my record- keeping if I could put down an exact cause of death. Kol Bjornlund overruled me — and the deceased's brother, as closest relative, took precedence."

"I see. Thanks, Chris."

"Any time, Thor. How's the wife?"

"Due in three weeks. Eric's hoping for a sister, believe it or not."

Dr. Stark laughed. "Good for him. Call again if I can answer any more questions about this, okay?"

"Will do. Bye." Nygaard tossed the receiver into its cradle and went to sit on Hafner's desk and tell him about the conversation. "I'm not sure there's anything in this," he concluded. "On the other hand, Mrs. Bjornlund seems damn sure something's wrong." He looked his notes over. "And if the body was found inside that high-tech house, how come Chris had to stop during his examination to use his hay fever medication?"

"Mr. Bjornlund probably got pollen or whatever all over his clothes during that walk in the yard," said Hafner. "I've got a friend who's so allergic to cats he can't go into a room where one has been sleeping, even if it isn't there any more."

"Helga said he'd never leave his house when it was dry and sunny, remember? And if he had enough pollen on his clothes to trigger an attack in the M.E., he must have not only gone for a walk, but been out there working in the flower beds. There's no mention of any dirt or sign of that. Anyway, he knew better." Nygaard frowned ponderously. "Maybe there is something fishy here."

Hafner knew that look. "Hey, now, slow down!" he said. "We've got enough of a caseload! There's that flasher, and the Geirson burglary, and what about the drug-dealing going on in the park? We're supposed to go out there this afternoon."

"Yeah, yeah," said Nygaard, waving a big paw dismissively. "Those pushers aren't going anywhere. You go talk to the brother; his name's Kol Bjornlund. He's the one who put the kibosh on the autopsy. I'll go see the niece, Anora. She's Kol's daughter; we'll see if their stories agree, okay?"

Kol Bjornlund reminded Hafner of a condor. He was bald and tall and very thin, with a jutting beak of a nose, small yellow eyes, and long wrinkled neck. He opened his arms a little in an expression of bewilderment and exasperation, and Hafner was almost surprised not to see feathers. "My brother is dead, Sergeant," he said. "He has been cremated and the ashes duly deposited in an urn which will be placed in a niche in Memorial Hall at the cemetery. Surely if there were any questions about his death, the time to have raised them has passed."

"Maybe," said Hafner, secretly agreeing with him. "Why did you object to an autopsy?"

"My brother had been in ill health for a number of years," said Kol. "He had a heart attack and died. Your medical examiner said that was the case. My daughter said, and I agreed, there was no reason to go poking about poor Ralph's innards in an attempt to confirm the obvious."

"You are the executor of the will?" asked Hafner.

"Yes."

"Would you mind telling me the extent of your brother's estate?"

"Yes, I do mind. I don't see that it's any of your business."

Hafner sighed. "We have received a complaint that your brother's death was suspicious, that in fact it was murder. If you choose to make it hard for us, the investigation will go on longer and you will be considerably bothered before we are finished with court orders and search warrants. I'm only trying to finish this up as quickly as I can. Your cooperation will speed the process, Mr. Bjornlund."

Kol fixed Hafner with a beady eye. "Very well," he said ungraciously. "The report is still being prepared for probate, but it should total about $800,000 — not including the house, which goes outright to my sister-in-law, Helga. I imagine she'll sell it; she has no need for a house that size. She also gets half of everything else. The rest is to be divided between myself and my daughter Anora. Anora receives the bigger share, and I the smaller. I might add that this is the fourth will my brother made in as many years. He quarreled with one or another of us frequently, and kept his lawyer busy redrafting the thing."

"So Anora's share will amount to — ?" Hafner paused inquiringly.

"Around a quarter of a million. I'll get perhaps a hundred fifty thousand, mostly in artwork. It's a shame Ralph died when he did; I'd been getting along with him to a degree lately, and I hear he'd quarreled with Helga."

Anora Bjornlund was slim to the point of delicacy above the waist, but had a sturdy peasant build below. Everything in her apartment seemed to be hand crafted, except the large gray cat which regarded Nygaard unwinkingly from a windowsill. There was a big loom in one corner, and she distracted Nygaard by constantly twirling a spindle during their conversation, feeding a thin twist of wool to it from a combed wad in her left hand.

"I began weaving when I was in high school," she said, smiling at him. Her hair was pale, increasing the impression of fragility. "I inherited some of my uncle's allergies, and spent a lot of time indoors."

"I see," said Nygaard. "How did you get along with your uncle?" he asked.

"Oh, sometimes well and other times not," she said, giving the wooden spindle another twirl. She was wearing a stiff jacket of some nubbly stuff over a denim skirt.

"What was your relationship at the time he died?"

"We were making up from a fight," she said. "It's always been harder to deal with him when he's right than when he's wrong. I wanted to give up my job as an art teacher and open a little shop to sell weaving materials and take commissions for special articles. He wouldn't give me the money to get started, so I borrowed some from the bank. Well, the shop failed, as he said it would, and he was perfectly insufferable about it. I got my job back at the university, swallowed my pride, and sent him a peace offering. Mr. Brodd was there when he got the package, and he said Uncle seemed quite touched." There was a little flare of pride in her pale eyes as she said this, and she stopped the spindle and began to wrap the new yarn around its shank.

"Had he quarreled with anyone else lately?"

"Yes, Aunt Helga. I don't know what it was about, but he'd sent for Mr. Brodd again." Her smile was malicious. "He's — he was poor uncle's long-suffering attorney. I suppose there have been four or five new wills in the past several years."

"What about your father? Did he get along with his brother?"

She twirled her spindle and began again to spin yarn. "Same as me: off and on. Although I believe their friendship was on again lately."

"You'd been out to visit your uncle recently?"

"Oh, no. The gift I sent him was just the first move in the peace negotiations. I hadn't seen him in person for over a year. Too bad he died; there's no telling how well we might have gotten along in future."

Over lunch Nygaard said, "Well, they agree Kol was getting along all right and Anora had opened a channel of communication with the old man." He took an enormous bite out of his hamburger. "How about you go see the lawyer – Harold Brodd – and I go see Helga and ask a few more questions?"

Hafner checked the interior of his ham and cheese for pickles – he didn't like pickles. "And which of us gets to explain to Captain Hamond why we haven't followed up on the Geirson burglary? No way, Thor. I told you before, we haven't got time for this wild goose chase, especially not when I have a very good lead on that burglar."

"All right, you go talk to the burglary victim. I'll go see Helga and Mr. Brodd both."

Harold Brodd was in his sixties, a vigorous silver-haired man, with an open, friendly, intelligent face. "The whole family is a pack of loons," he said with a short laugh. "And Ralph Bjornlund was not the worst of them."

"Who was the worst?" asked Nygaard, settling back in the comfortable leather chair in the attorney's office.

"Anora, probably. Her name should have been Arachne, after the spider. Spinning and weaving her life away – oh, she's got talent; I've seen some very fine things come off her loom or away from her knitting needles. But then she'll turn around and make ugly, lumpish wall hangings or stuff that looks like low-grade burlap. And she's a sucker for any sociologic fad that comes along. Transactional analysis, tarot, primal scream, herbal teas, sensory deprivation – I hear she's into rune stones now."

"Do you know anything about her making up her quarrel with her Uncle Ralph?"

"Oh, yes. She sent him a hand-knitted sweater – not of wool, he was allergic to wool. She made the supreme sacrifice and knitted it in orlon. Her loom probably wouldn't speak to her for a week. Ralph had invited me to lunch, and the sweater came in the mail while I was there. He opened the package and looked at it, and actually seemed touched. He was a very peculiar old man, you know. Short tempered and cruel most of the time, but eventually ready to make up and try again."

"Maybe he felt close to Anora because she'd inherited his allergies."

"Not all of them. Pollen bothered her, and chocolate. I used to tease her that her complexion was so clear because she never ate chocolate. But eggs were okay. Good thing, too; being able to eat eggs sustained her through her six months as a vegetarian."

"What's your opinion of Anora's father?"

"Kol? Well, it's from him she got the Bjornlund tendency to lunacy. But his comes out in spite and meanness, as it did in his brother. Not that she's not spiteful, but she's more goofy than anything. Kol could carry a grudge better than Ralph, and he had more of the family tendency to greediness. But he's not vicious and crafty, at least not as much as the rest of them."

"How about Helga?"

"Oh, she's all right. She only married into the Bjornlund line. Her husband, Sven Bjornlund, was the baby of the family. He died of cancer ten or twelve years ago, but she stayed close to the other two. She always got along better with Ralph and Kol than Sven did anyway. A bit opinionated and more stubborn than you'd think on seeing what a sweet-looking old thing she is. Not vicious like the real Bjornlunds are, but a whole lot smarter."

Nygaard found Helga in her greenhouse, dabbing a flower with a small, soft brush. There was a strong odor of earth and growing things, muggier and more pungent than the spring air outdoors. As he watched, she walked a little way down the row, and dabbed the brush onto another flower. What was she doing? wondered Nygaard. Killing aphids, maybe? Treating some kind of plant disease? He started towards her and she caught his movement out of the corner of her eye. "Oh, hello, Sergeant Nygaard," she said, turning and putting the brush into her apron pocket. "Have you brought me some news of poor Ralph?"

"No, not yet," said Nygaard. "But I have come to interview you, if that's all right."

"Certainly, certainly. Come with me." She led the way to her tiny office between the greenhouse and her retail store. She pulled off cotton gloves as she sat down. "What do you want to ask me?"

"First, what were you doing in there?"

"Pollinating. Bees are so careless, you know. This way I know who the parents of my seedlings are."

He chuckled. "I see. Did you know Ralph Bjornlund was about to make a new will?"

She smiled sadly. "I suspected it. He generally did when quarrels got serious or went on a long time."

"What had you quarreled with him about?"

She sighed. "My greenhouse. He wanted me to give it up and come be his live-in housekeeper. He was always afraid I'd come and visit him right after working with my flowers, without changing clothes, and set off an attack. He said I was getting old and forgetful." She shrugged at Nygaard. "Now I can't deny I'm getting on, but I don't think I'm in the least senile. Anyway, I didn't want to come live with him. He's never kept a housekeeper longer than six months, and I couldn't believe it would be any different with me." She stopped, amused. "So in order not to set myself up for a quarrel with him, I quarreled with him. Maybe he was right, maybe I'm getting soft in the head."

Nygaard didn't think so. "Who in the family was most in need of money?"

She thought about that. "Anora, I suppose. She has no head for money, poor thing, and she was getting seriously behind in paying back that bank loan. She'd had to give up her car and move to a smaller apartment. Her salary isn't very large, you know. Her father couldn't help; Kol's never been able to handle money either, so he's got everything tied up in annuities and trusts. He's retired, of course. He was an engineer like his brother, only not nearly as successful. That pollen counter outside Ralph's window was Kol's idea, you know. In fact, the device is his prototype. He sold the design to Ralph for next to nothing, poor old goof. Though Ralph did say it needed considerable work."

"Did the device work?" asked Nygaard.

"I don't know. Kol was over tinkering with it a few days before Ralph died. I think he was hoping Ralph would let him buy back a half interest in it or something."

"If Kol is so bad with money, why weren't you named executor?"

"Why, because I'm a woman!" She chuckled drily. "Ralph always suspected I had a secret partner, male, who helped me with my business; he simply couldn't believe a female was capable of adding a column of figures and getting the same answer twice. He thought Anora's fiscal problems arose out of her sex, but I think it was because she was a Bjornlund."

"But Ralph could handle money, right?"

"No, not really. He had several very basic patents in clean room technology, and with the income they generated, it didn't matter if he occasionally invested in bad stocks or real estate that turned out to be desert or swamp."

"Do you think Anora was really on the verge of making up that quarrel?"

"Possibly. She came crying to me about it, and together we worked out the idea of a handmade gift. Ralph liked women who baked cookies or sewed dresses − he put up with me because he considered me at bottom only a fancy sort of flower arranger − and I suggested she knit something for him. She was very grateful for my help, and even brought the sweater to me for approval before she sent it. It was a lovely thing, beautifully done. Ralph was wearing it the day he died."

"So you saw it before she sent it?"

"Oh, yes. I borrowed it for a day to show a friend, hoping to generate an order. Anora still takes orders." She cocked her head and looked at him appraisingly. "You'd look nice in a Norwegian sweater, Sergeant, with those big shoulders of yours."

Nygaard grinned, abashed. "Thank you, ma'am."

He called Dr. Stark when he got back to the office. "You say you had an asthma attack when you were examining Ralph Bjornlund's body?"

"An allergic reaction of some sort, yes."

"If he'd brushed up against something full of pollen while out in his yard, could that have set off a reaction in you?"

"Yes; in fact, that's what I think happened."

"What happened to the clothes he was wearing when you found him?"

"I don't know, Thor. He didn't end up in my autopsy room, remember? Call Steinkel's, they took him away."

Nygaard called the Steinkel Funeral Home and asked Mr. Steinkel, "What happened to the clothes the late Ralph Bjornlund was wearing when he died? Was he cremated in them?"

Steinkel said, faintly shocked, "No, of course not. We put him into one of our special ultralight suits and featherweight slumber shoes for visitation, and he was cremated in those. The clothing he was wearing at the time of his demise was returned to Mr. Kol Bjornlund along with the cremains."

"Thank you, sir," Nygaard said, and went to tell Hafner, "I think I've got it." But Jack didn't have time for talk. He had nabbed the Geirson burglar a few hours earlier, and was up to his ears in paperwork, preparing the file for the County Prosecutor.

"His clothing? Well, I don't know. Wait, yes, I do. It's at the house. Why?" Kol's condor face was suspicious.

"I'd like them subjected to certain tests by our forensics lab," said Nygaard.

"What kind of tests?"

"Nothing that will harm the clothing, I promise. I want to see if we can prove your brother took a walk in his garden the morning of his death."

"Chris, what would happen if someone dusted pollen all over a sweater before presenting it to you as a gift?"

"I'd burn it," said Dr. Stark.

"No, suppose you didn't know he'd done it?"

"It wouldn't take me long to find out; I'd start wheezing and choking."

"And if you had a weak heart?"

"What are you getting at?"

"Here's the sweater Ralph Bjornlund was wearing when he died. Can you check it for pollen?"

"Right now?"

"Yes, right now. While I look over your shoulder." Nygaard had an intense way about him when hot on some trail; Stark sighed and unfolded the sweater. He went to his desk, opened a drawer and shut it again, opened another, and shut it. "I'm out of Scotch Tape."

"What do you want tape for?"

"To lift particles of dust or pollen off the sweater. Wait here, I'll go borrow some."

"Can't you just pull out a few fibers and look at them under a microscope?" Nygaard asked impatiently.

Stark sighed again and went to a counter cluttered with equipment, including two microscopes. He used a pair of tweezers to pull loose some fibers from the sweater and teased them onto a slide. The slide was put under a microscope and a strong light turned on. Stark bent and looked. He shifted the slide's position a time or two, then straightened. "No pollen I can see," he reported.

"Try another sample, up near the neckline, in front." In his mind's eye Nygaard could see Helga in her greenhouse, and he smelled murder.

Stark repeated his procedure with the tweezers and bent again over the microscope. "No, no pollen here, either. Look, I've got some other things to – to do – arou – ACHOO!"

"There, see?" said Nygaard. "Look again."

Stark blew his nose and tried again. Nothing.

"But you're having a reaction, aren't you?"

"So?" said Stark thickly. "I'm allergic to other things, you know."

"Like what?"

"Cats. Eggs. Gold."

A new image rose up in Nygaard's mind. "What's that sweater made of?"

"Couple things. Some artificial fiber and something natural, too. I saw it in the second sample, from the gray section."

"Wool, maybe?"

"Huh-uh, I don't think so. Anyway, wool makes me itch, not sneeze. Lemme look again."

The second slide was put onto a different microscope, one with two stages and a selection of sample fibers was tried on the other stage. "Cat," said Stark a few minutes later. "Well, by God," he added, turning to stare at Nygaard. "That's wha – wha – ACHOO!"

"She was getting a cool quarter million by the terms of the current will," said Nygaard. "More than enough to pay off the loan and try again with another shop. It might have taken months to conclude the making-up process with her uncle, with no guarantee there wouldn't immediately be another quarrel — or that he would favor her over her father in any future will. She was in serious financial difficulty; she needed the money now. And being number two was safer. I was looking long and hard at Helga simply because she had the most to gain by the terms of the current will."

"How come Ralph didn't see cat hairs all over his new sweater? Surely he knew Anora had a cat; I'd've thought he'd look for them," said Hafner.

"They weren't on the surface," said Nygaard. "They were the gray pattern. She saved combings from her cat, spun them into yarn, and knitted the yarn into the sweater. Then she went to Helga and helped her suggest a handmade gift might soften her old uncle's heart."

"Can you do that with cat hair — turn it into yarn?"

"Oh, yes; there was a fad for it for awhile among weavers, saving pet hair and turning it into hats and sweaters. I found an article about it in a craft magazine Anora had saved."

"She give you any problem about a search?"

"No, once I told her she was under arrest she seemed relieved, and barely waited until I finished warning her before she told me all about it. She was pretty proud of her plan — and it was slick, you know."

"Slick ladies with her moral sense belong in jail," said Hafner drily.

"I agree; I hope she gets my sweater finished before she comes to trial," said Nygaard.

"Sweater? You're not letting her — " began Hafner, and stopped, too indignant to continue.

"Why not? I'm not allergic to anything. It was Judy's idea. She's paying for it, she says its my birthday present. It'll be gray, with a cream and red starburst pattern." He wrapped a big paw around his coffee mug and took a sip, thinking. "You know, after the trial I may order one for Judy, and maybe one for Eric, for Christmas. And when the new one starts to walk, we'll get one for her. Or him. Because come to think of it, I'll know where to send the order — and she'll be there a long, long time."

Hafner stared at his partner. "You are a loony tune, you know that?"

"You think so? You didn't see the sweater she knitted for her uncle, Jack. She's a talented lady. And like you pointed out with Eric's fish, it will help to have something to point to when I tell this story to my friends in years to come. It may even become an heirloom."

Hafner snorted. "Hair-loom, you mean!"

"*Uff da!*" groaned Nygaard, and began to laugh.

THE SCALES OF JUSTICE

"Grimby, bring us another deck, will you?" asked Nygaard when the deal came to him. "I've been drawing too many runts with this one."

"Sure, Thor."

Nygaard opened the box, removed the jokers and shuffled thoroughly. Pederson cut and Nygaard announced, "Five card draw, five dollar limit on raises − " He was approaching the sum he would allow himself to lose and did not want to be forced out of the game just yet − "nothing wild. Ante up."

Larry Fields was new to their friendly game − vouched for by Ken Olson, desk clerk at the Valhalla Inn. They hadn't completely taken his measure yet. His mannerisms seemed to gain new vigor with this game. He fiddled incessantly with his cards, rearranging their order again and again. He pursed his lips and whistled softly, glanced at the other players frequently, and when he caught Nygaard's eye on him, he began to break down and restack his chips with an air of impatience. Not impatience to bet; he stayed with apparent reluctance, not raising. When Nygaard called for discards, Fields pulled three random cards from his hand. "Three, please," he said, tossing them down.

"Give me two good ones," begged Balstad.

"One," said Draxten soberly.

"I'll take three," yipped Pederson bossily.

"And dealer takes two," said Nygaard, handing around replacements. "What do you bet, Larry?"

Fields picked up some chips without looking, counting them as he dropped them into the middle. "One, two, three, four dollars," he said, and began again to rearrange the cards in his hand.

"Possible straight, possible flush: Nothing," growled Balstad, putting his cards down. "I fold."

"I'm in," said Pederson, adding his four chips to the pot.

Draxten said, "Eight," raising the bet four dollars.

Nygaard saw the eight and raised five. He had barely any idea of what was in his hand; he was too busy keeping covert eyes on Fields' every fidget. "Up to you, Larry," he said.

Fields glanced at Nygaard, then at Draxten. "Oh, I think I'll fold, okay?" He closed his cards like a fan and dropped them.

"I'll see Thor's five and − " began Pederson.

"Hold it," said Nygaard. He reached out and picked up Field's cards, including his previous discards. "I want to take a look at something."

"Hey, you can't do that; the hand isn't over!" said Pederson.

"It's against the rules to look at a folded hand," agreed Balstad.

"Which rules? Ours, or the ones this joker's been playing by?" The atmosphere in the room abruptly altered.

"Careful, Thor," cautioned Draxten.

"You'd better not be saying what I think you're saying," blustered Fields.

Nygaard called across the room, "Grimby, where's our old deck?"

Grimby, looking fiercely suspicious, went behind the bar and produced it.

Nygaard took the old deck and went quickly through it, pulling out the aces and face cards. He handed them to Balstad. "Mark, shuffle these and lay them out face down on the table for me."

"Sure, all right. But I hope to God you know what you're doing." Balstad riffled them a couple of times and laid them out on Nygaard's side of the pot.

Meanwhile, Nygaard examined the cards Fields had handled in this last hand. "You threw away an ace, jack, queen I see," he said. "That wasn't very bright."

"So?" said Fields, but he sounded wary.

"And you drew another queen. And a ten and a trey."

"Yeah, I kept my two hearts; I was after a flush, see?"

The players frowned; that was so stupid even a beginner wouldn't do it.

Nygaard turned the ace, jack and queens over and got very interested in their backs; and then in the long edges of the cards from the old deck. After awhile he straightened and smiled. "Want to see a magic trick?" he asked. He reached out and touched the backs of four cards in the set Pederson had laid out. "Those are the queens," he said, and turned them over to prove himself correct.

"Jesus sufferin' Christ!" exclaimed Balstad.

Nygaard said to Fields, "All those wriggles and fussing were to cover your marking the cards, right? And you switched from fooling with your cards to fooling with your chips whenever you saw me paying attention to you."

"You're a goddam liar!" said Fields.

"Am I? I noticed you started folding whenever the dealer called some cards wild — you couldn't read a fistful of wild cards, could you? There wasn't going to be time to mark all the cards, so you marked only the face cards — and the aces," said Nygaard, and he turned over four more cards from the old deck, all aces.

Pederson yapped, "Cheat! You lousy cheater!"

"Don't say cheat to me!" said Fields. "He's the one who can read the cards from the back!"

"No, sir," said Nygaard, "that dog won't bark. This is a new deck, and I learned how to read the marks from the cards you were holding, cards I held only long enough to put in front of you and never saw the faces of."

"How do you read them, Thor?" asked Balstad.

"Look here, see these little notches on the edges of the cards? Aces notched near the top, kings down a bit, queens further down, and jacks near the middle. I think we should take a look at his fingernails to see if one is filed sharp, or maybe at that big ring he's wearing, to see if it's got a raised edge on its underside."

Fields stood, his face a deep red. "This is some kind of stickup, isn't it? You'll pretend to find a rough spot and keep the ring. Well, you won't get away with it! This is a nine-hundred-dollar ring, and if you take it away from me, I'll have the law on you, see if I don't!"

For some reason, this made everyone in the room laugh. "What's so stinkin' funny?" demanded Fields.

Nygaard, grinning fiercely, said, "Maybe we should introduce ourselves again. I'm detective sergeant Thor Nygaard, Hedeby police. The man with the red sweater is Mark Balstad, our county prosecutor. Nils Pederson, the yappy one there, is about as good a criminal defense lawyer as Hedeby has. And the big, sad-eyed cuss, the man with the second-highest pile of chips, is Tillman Draxten, Judge of District Court."

Fields' deep color faded to a pasty white. "What kind of crazy town is this?" he demanded. Even louder, "And so what? This is still an illegal game!"

"Yeah, we know," said Nygaard. "That's why we have to hide out in old Grimby's basement whenever we want to play it."

"Well, then you know you can't arrest a man for cheating in an illegal game of chance."

"He's right, you know," Prosecutor Balstad said. "I would never bring him into court."

"And if he did, I could defend him with one hand tied behind my back," added Attorney Pederson.

"And I'd dismiss the charges," said Judge Draxten.

"There, see?" said Fields. "So you caught me, so what? Take my winnings, give me the hundred and fifty I came in with, and I'll be on my way." He began to reach for his chips.

But a large hand seized his wrist in a mighty grip. Fields dropped the blue chips he had picked up, twisted around and saw the largest man in the room looming over him.

"Keep your fat hands off the table!" Nygaard said.

"Haul him out in back and rough him up some, Thor," suggested Grimby, who had gone behind his bar for a child's baseball bat. He let it smack into the palm of one hand. "I'll help, if you want me to."

Fields snarled, "All right, all right; keep all the money! It's highway robbery, but keep the money! Now let go!"

"No," said Nygaard. He was very angry, his clenched face threateningly close to Fields'.

"Hold it," growled Draxten, with his judge's authority. The others looked at him. "Let's not be hasty, or do something illegal. The man is a cheat, obviously. However, he's been caught before he made away with our money. I think we should separate him from that amount he won from us by cheating and ship him off. What do you think, Mr. Balstad?"

"Sounds fair to me."

"I think we should sit him down and make him eat those marked cards!" said Pederson.

Draxten consulted his watch. "We haven't got time for that. It's after six and we have to be at the lodge by seven-thirty in good bib and tucker."

Balstad stood. "Is it as late as that?" He lived well outside of town, and the snowy roads would slow travel. He began to gather his chips. "Cash me in, Nils. You guys will have to decide what to do with our friend here without my help. Fine him everything he's got on the table and let him go; that's my advice." He changed his chips into forty-seven dollars in cash and left.

"Don't do anything to him that will leave a mark," advised Pederson the lawyer. "Or he might sue."

"That money on the table," said Fields, "is all the money I've got."

"No it isn't," said Nygaard. "There's plenty more cash in your wallet; I saw it when you bought in the second time. And you've got more credit cards than the rest of us put together."

"Just once," said Grimby. "Hit him just one time. Or let me hit him."

"Shut up, Grimby – and you, let him go, Thor," said Draxten, putting on his coat. "Cash me in, Nils."

"Think of something mean, legal and appropriate to do to him and I will."

"I don't want any part of that, thank you," said Draxten. "If you can think of something yourself, be my guest. Nils, if you want a ride home, you'll have to leave with me now."

Pederson hesitated, torn. "Oh, all right," he said. "Here's your money. Thor, let me know what you decide, okay?"

"Sure."

Pederson left with Draxten. Then, except for Grimby, Nygaard was alone in the basement room with his captive.

"Grimby, can I use your phone?" Nygaard asked.

"Sure. Are you going to hit him or not?"

"Naw, I'm so mad I might accidentally kill him. Then there'd be a stink."

"Hide him outdoors, and he won't stink until next spring," said Grimby grinning. But he decided Nygaard wasn't going to do anything worth watching, at least right then, so he said, "I got to go shower and change for the dinner. See you there?"

"Yeah," said Nygaard absently, hanging on to Fields with one hand and dialing with the other. "Hello, Jack? It's me, Thor."

Jack Hafner was Nygaard's partner in the squad room, and a cool head. However, when he heard Nygaard's complaint, he only laughed. "I'm with the judge on this one, Thor," he said. "I don't think there's anything you can do but turn him loose."

Nygaard said something rude about Jack's lack of imagination and hung up. He said to Fields, "Maybe I should put you outside in your stocking feet. And drop your car keys down a storm drain, if I could find one under the snow."

"You do that, or leave any kind of mark of violence on me," threatened Fields, "and by God, I'll go to your newspaper with the story of this poker setup you've got here, and everyone will suffer."

"Those would be serious charges," agreed Nygaard, considering the threat. "And there'd be an investigation. We'd have to hold you as a material witness. And who knows how long it would take to bring in an outside judge?"

Fields grinned, "Yeah, but in the end you'd lose your badge. I think we got us a Mexican standoff here." Fields offered a carrot. "Look, keep the money. In fact, let me add fifty dollars to it. You don't have to share it; you can always say you gave it back to me. I'll leave town tonight, I promise, and no one will ever know."

"An offer of bribery is even stupider than trying to cheat us," Nygaard said, his fjord-blue eyes taking on a frosty paleness. He picked up the money and put it in his pocket for later distribution. "You're leaving all right," he added, "and I want to make sure you never come back." The ambiguity of this statement reduced Fields to a frightened silence.

"Thor, for Pete's sake, you can't bring him in here!" hissed Balstad. "For one thing, he hasn't got a ticket! And for another, he isn't Norwegian!"

"Hush up, Mark, okay? He's my guest. We're allowed to bring a guest to a lodge dinner, aren't we? And since Judy's working in the kitchen tonight, I'm bringing my buddy Mr. Fields along." He grinned down at the man, large teeth shining. "It'll give me more time to think of something mean, appropriate and maybe even legal."

Fields had given up arguing. He looked tired and a little depressed; even the diamond in his ring seemed dim. Nygaard had taken him to his home and handcuffed him to the refrigerator while showering and changing, and driven him to the lodge hall at a rate of speed Fields had privately considered far too fast for road conditions. Nygaard was now acting more out of stubbornness than anger, Fields knew. But Fields recalled the look in the big man's eye when he offered the bribe, and did not care to inadvertently rekindle that look.

The elevator door slid open, and the smell of something warm and damp rolled in.

"What the hell is that?" said Fields, hanging back.

"What?" asked Nygaard, pulling him out of the elevator.

"That smell."

"What smell?"

"It's lutefisk," said Balstad, uncovering his curls as if in a gesture of respect. He inhaled greedily. "Torsk."

"Torsk?"

"That's Norwegian for cod."

"Come on, this way," said Nygaard impatiently. He led them down a hallway to a door guarded by a pleasant-faced woman counting dollar bills and putting rubber bands around little stacks of them.

"Well, hello, Thor Nygaard," she said. "I was wondering if you'd get here on time." There was an odd lilt in her voice, as if it were carried on little waves.

"Inga, how could I not be here, knowing you'd be at the door to greet me?" He showed her a yellow pasteboard ticket.

She blushed and waved dismissively at him. "Go on with you," she said. "And save that for the drawing next week."

"Any tickets left?"

She looked in her metal box. "Yes, three or four."

"Good, my friend wants some real old-fashioned Norwegian food."

Nygaard nudged Fields, who reached for his wallet. "How much?" he asked.

"Seven dollars, fifty cents," she said. He paid her, and was rewarded with a yellow ticket. "What's your last name?" she asked curiously.

"Fields."

"Oh, then it's your mother who's from Norway?"

"No – uh, yes," he amended, as he felt another massive nudge. "Uh – Johannsen was her name."

She frowned. "Johannsen is Swedish, isn't it?"

"Uh, yeah, but they moved to Norway before she was born."

"Ah, then welcome to Tofte Lodge," she smiled, and handed him his change.

"Thank you," said Fields.

The room was crowded with people, many of them tall, most of them fair, quite a few carrying frosty glasses that tinkled refreshingly. Fields noticed a bar in the corner. "I could use a drink," he hinted, but Nygaard was looking for familiar faces, and greeting them with waves and grins.

A big man with a huge red mustache confronted Nygaard and said belligerently through a haze of whiskey fumes, "I hear we're gonna have to discontinue our 911 emergency phone number."

"Why's that, Sven?" asked Nygaard.

"'Cause none of us Norwegians can find eleven on the dial!"

Fields braced himself for an explosion, but when it came, it was laughter. Thor slapped the man on his shoulder and shouted, "Haw, haw haw! I'll have to remember that one!" He nudged Fields who give an obliging and puzzled chuckle.

A very proper looking young woman came by and told a surprisingly raunchy joke involving Ole and Lena, which again insulted Norwegians. And again Nygaard laughed his big laugh.

Fields waited until the young woman went away, and asked, "If you're all Norwegians, how come you're not telling German jokes? Or whatever."

"Danish jokes," said Nygaard. "Sometimes we tell Danish jokes. But mostly we tell jokes on ourselves."

"I don't get it."

"Well, we'd tell Polish jokes," said Nygaard, "except we don't understand them." And he laughed his great haw, haw, haw. Still grinning, Nygaard looked down at Fields. "You know, you look sorta like a guy the police in International Falls are looking for. Maybe I should keep you down at the jail until he can come down and check it out, which could take four or five days if the snow keeps up like the weatherman says it might. That would be legal."

Fields ventured a suggestion that that might constitute false arrest.

"Naw, more like mistaken identity, I think. Of course, on the other hand, if Tommy Olson has to come all the way down here on a false alarm, he's gonna be mad at me. And if he stays mad, he might not let me use his cabin in the Boundary Waters next summer. And what would I do if I couldn't fish for walleyes in the Boundary Waters?" With a massive, regretful sigh, Nygaard dropped that idea. He renewed his grip on the unfortunate gambler's arm, and they worked their way slowly toward the double doors at the back of the reception area. The smell of something that had been forcibly removed from the sea, and cruelly treated besides, grew stronger.

Fields murmured apologetically, "I really don't much care for fish." As if in sympathy, a low moaning sound filled the room and stilled all conversation.

"There goes the lur-horn," said Nygaard happily. "Let's eat!"

The dining hall was very large, and its two longer walls were lined with thin horizontal slats of wood that curved upwards at one end, giving the impression the room was inside an enormous longboat. Several dozen tables covered with white paper tablecloths filled the floor. On an unslatted wall straight ahead was a big American flag flanked by two Norwegian flags, which in turn were flanked by murderous-looking battle-axes crossed behind brass-knobbed shields.

"Everybody in town must be Norwegian, to support a place this big," said Fields.

"Yeah, there's a lot of us all right," said Nygaard, leading Fields to a table near the front. "Say, do you sell snowmobile suits?"

"No, of course not!"

"Then what are you doing in Minnesota? Snowmobile suits are practically a winter uniform up here. What kind of a sporting goods company do you work for, anyhow?"

"A very good sporting goods company." Fields smelled − in addition to the fish − another of Nygaard's screwball plans in the making. "Are you in the market for a snowmobile suit?"

"No, I got one. But you spoiled my next plan. I was thinking, suppose your luggage accidentally got mixed up with someone else's? And it got put on the bus Valhalla runs up to the Twin Cities international airport. And ended up in, say, Cancun, Mexico? You might be grateful for a snowmobile suit to wear until the airline got your luggage back."

"How would you get hold of my luggage without breaking into my hotel room? The management might not think much of that.

They might put a lot of pressure on the police department to solve the burglary."

"Yeah, they might at that," said Nygaard, and Fields offered an inaudible sigh of relief.

They took seats at a table near the flagged wall, set for six with white china plates and thick coffee mugs. The smell of fish was now very strong indeed. Nygaard waved an arm over his head, and they were joined by Judge Draxten and his wife, a tiny lady with grey eyes and hair.

"I would have thought you'd have gotten rid of Mr. Fields by now," said Draxten, as they sat down.

"Tillman, what a rude thing to say!" said Mrs. Draxten. "I think it was very kind of Sergeant Nygaard to bring him along for a taste of old-country cooking."

"Hamburgers would've been fine," muttered Fields, not quietly enough. A massive elbow nudged his ribs and he added hastily, "But I'm looking forward to an interesting meal."

There was an electronic shriek, and all eyes turned to the front of the room, where a podium stood in a spotlight under the American flag. A tall man with golden hair was adjusting the microphone. Beside him stood a tiny girl in a pink dress.

"Hello!" he said, and his voice was broadcast with ear-shattering faithfulness to the farthest reaches of the room. Hands flew to ears. He frowned, and when he spoke again, his voice had been reduced to a scant whisper. His lips moved, and they heard, at a near-proper volume, " . . . two, three, testing, one, two. There, that's better. Welcome to the Tofte Lodge Lutefisk Dinner. The cooks inform me all is in readiness, so without further ado, I will present little Astrid, who will recite for us." He bent and lifted the child, whose hair was so fair it glowed almost white under the spotlight. She clutched the microphone, pulling herself horizontal, then saw how many eyes were one her and lost her nerve.

"Go on, honey," called someone from a table near her, and she rewarded him with a shy smile.

"Okay," she said, took a deep breath and recited all in a rush, "*I Jesus' Navn gar gi til bords, Spider, drikker pa dit ord, Dig til aere, od til gavn, Sa far vi mat i Jesus' Navn.*"

Fields suddenly realized he was the only one in the room whose head was not bowed. They were saying grace, he realized, and when Nygaard nudged him, he said "Amen," loudly.

Their waiter came by and put two platters on the table, one stacked with whitish squares, thin and limp; the other piled with pale freckled rectangles the size of graham crackers.

"Flatbread," said Nygaard, picking up one of the cracker-like rectangles. "Made of oatmeal. Try one."

Fields tasted a piece. Its texture was rather like cardboard found under a bush after a long winter, but it didn't taste bad.

The limp things didn't taste bad either, nor good; they had virtually no taste at all. "Lefse, potato bread," Mrs. Draxten said as she showed him how to fold it into a triangle and spread butter on it. "A little sugar is good, too," she counseled, sprinkling some on hers.

Fields copied her, and agreed it improved the flavor. His spirits rose a little. This might not be such a bad meal after all.

"Obviously your mother didn't do much Norwegian cooking at your house," Mrs. Draxten said.

"No, ma'am."

"Too bad," said Nygaard. "No one prepares fish like the Scandinavians do."

"Which is probably why our ancestors went a-Viking," said a voice behind them.

"Jack!" said Nygaard, turning in his chair.

Hafner, a trimly built man with dark hair and gray eyes, stood smiling down at them. "May I have this empty chair, or are you saving it for someone?" he asked.

"Sit, sit down!" said Nygaard.

Hafner sat and grinned. "And you would be Mr. Fields? I thought Thor would have sent you on your way by now."

"No, I haven't," said Nygaard. "Not yet. Maybe I should take him to a tattoo parlor to get a shark tattooed onto the back of each of his hands. Or would that be leaving a mark?"

Hafner laughed and Mrs. Draxten asked, "Why a shark?"

Judge Draxten said, "He's a card shark; we caught him cheating at poker this afternoon."

Mrs. Draxten fixed Fields with an eye turned the color of a winter sea. "I hope you are ashamed of yourself, sir," she said.

"Well, I suppose I am," said Fields, glancing in Nygaard's direction.

A waiter in a dark suit carefully lowered an enormous platter piled high with slabs of something that smelled of old fishing nets onto the place of honor at the center of the table. The lutefisk had arrived. Nygaard deftly captured the biggest piece for himself, and courteously insisted Fields take the second-biggest.

Hafner asked, "What do you know about lutefisk, Mr. Fields?"

Fields, frowning at the quivering whiteness on his plate, replied, "Not a thing."

"It's an interesting food, made from ocean cod. Goes back at least to medieval times, before refrigeration. After the fish is caught, it's salted down, then dried. It can last for months that way. When you get a taste for fish and it's too cold to go fishing, you bring out the lutefisk. But it's stiff as a board, so you soak it in a lye bath to soften it up. That breaks down the tissue and melts the bones right into jelly. When you can feel your fingers with your thumb right through a slab of fish, it's almost ready. Then put it in fresh water for a day or two to get rid of the lye, boil it a few hours just to make sure it's really soft, and serve it up just like you see it here. Nice, huh? That piece of fish on you plate there was caught last summer and never saw a refrigerator in its life."

"No kidding," said Fields, looking at the very large chunk of lutefisk on his plate. Beside him, Nygaard was pouring melted butter over his portion. Nygaard was not denying the description, not breaking into his big haw, haw, haw to show this was a joke.

"Delicious!" said Thor, forking away a huge mouthful. "Eat up, Larry!" Fields felt a big elbow land in his ribs.

He took a small bite and discovered the questionable pleasures of fish-flavored jelly. "Pass the butter, please," he said miserably.

"Here come the potatoes!" said Nygaard. Norwegian style potatoes are boiled until they begin to break apart, then shaken in a colander until they are dry and mealy. But they are not treated with lye and don't taste of fish. Fields took two, anxious to clear his palate.

Another bowl arrived. "Ah, the mashed rutabaga," said Hafner, "cooked in pork-flavored milk."

Before Fields could say, "None for me please," Nygaard had put a large dollop on his plate.

"You get your money's worth at Tofte Lodge!" Nygaard said cheerfully, taking an enormous serving for himself. "Eat, Larry; you may never get a meal like this again."

Fields, with a staggering effort, ate most of his fish and half his rutabagas. "I — I guess I'm not very hungry," he said when he saw Nygaard's censuring eye.

"I'm not surprised," said Mrs. Draxten. "Sitting here among all these nice people. You belong in jail."

"Sergeant Nygaard suggested that, but I'm afraid I talked him out of it," sighed Fields.

Nygaard glanced over and said, "I knew you'd like it once you tried it; here, have some more lutefisk." He put another piece on Fields' plate with the careless largess of a man who has already paid for all he can eat. He added a slab to his own plate and reached for the little pitcher of melted butter. It was a fresh pitcher, and hot, and he dropped it hard enough to spill a molten puddle onto the paper tablecloth. "*Uff da!*" he said.

"*Uff da?*" said Fields.

Hafner explained, "If a Norwegian were taking out the garbage and the bottom fell out of the bag onto his good shoes, he'd say '*uff da*.' If he came home to find his wife had run off with the milkman, he'd say '*uff da*.' If he heard on the radio that an armed nuclear warhead had been accidentally launched and would land in his back yard in thirty seconds, he'd say '*uff da*.'"

Everyone laughed, and Nygaard said, "I'd run for the hills, but you're right; I'd mutter '*uff da*' all the way. C'mon, Larry, you're falling behind! Eat, eat!"

Buying time, Fields pointed at a series of wooden roundels on the wall. "What do the words on the blue one mean?" He wished Nygaard would leave him alone; he felt one more bite would make him break out in soft, white scales. If only the man weren't so big. The worst part was that Nygaard thought he was being nice. If this was nice, God save him from whatever Nygaard considered justice — much less the vengeance he was so hopped up on.

Mrs. Draxten looked at the roundels on the wall. "'*Smuler er ogsaa brod*,'" she said, and paused to translate in her head. "That means, 'Crumbs are also bread.'"

Fields frowned at her. "Does it have some other kind of meaning?"

She turned back to him. "It means what it says, Mr. Fields."

"Well, it seems a trifle obvi — " He broke off and rolled a nervous eye at Nygaard. "I mean, that doesn't seem to be, er, very significant, considering all the work someone did to hang it up there." The lettering was fancy, and the roundel was decorated with white and yellow flowers.

She was looking puzzled at his obtuseness. "It means, when we pray for our daily bread, we should be thankful even if all we get is crumbs, Mr. Fields."

"Yeah, like I may have to settle for just punching you in the nose one time," said Nygaard, and he laughed his big laugh. Fields looked at Nygaard's hands and winced. Maybe if he stood and very quickly smashed his chair over the big cop's thick, stupid, blond head — No, that was his partner sitting right there. Cops tended to carry their guns all the time, and God knew what kind of a shot these two were. Nygaard cast a glance at him, and he took a large bite of lutefisk. Bad as it was, the rutabagas were worse.

"Ah, dessert!" said Nygaard at last, and he gratefully put down his fork. Even Norwegians couldn't come up with something truly awful for dessert, could they?

"Prune compote!" said the irrepressible Hafner.

"Uh — " said Fields, but Nygaard was too quick for him.

"You'll want a lot of this," said Nygaard. "Seeing how little of everything else you ate."

"No, really; just a bit!" pleaded Fields, but Nygaard loaded his plate with a second large spoonful.

Hafner began to laugh. When Nygaard turned a bewildered face to him, he laughed harder. "Too much, too much!" he choked, between spasms, tapping his enormous friend on the shoulder.

Nygaard handed him the bowl of compote and asked, "Are you all right, Jack?"

"I'm fine!" said Hafner, handing on the bowl and going into fresh peals.

"Come on, pal, what's the joke?" asked Nygaard impatiently.

Surprised but still laughing, Hafner asked, "You mean you honestly don't know?"

"Know what?"

"Your punishment for your cheatin' buddy over there," said Hafner. "I never would've though you'd come up with something so sneaky as that."

"What, sneaky?" demanded Nygaard, beginning to sound annoyed.

"Come on, you seriously think all an outsider has to do is taste lutefisk to be converted to the Norwegian way of taste? You've been tearing down this poor geek shingle by shingle all evening! Bringing him to the dinner and filling him up with lutefisk, rutabagas and prune compote, ha, ha, ha! Mean and legal and doesn't leave a mark, just like you wanted!" He saw the honest bewilderment on his partner's face and laughed even harder. "Oh, God, you thought you were doing him a favor, didn't you?"

"What favor?" asked Nygaard angrily. "I made him pay for his ticket!" This set everyone at the table off.

Nygaard turned to look at Fields, and saw, for the first time, the greenish pallor and glazed eyes. "Well, double my IQ and call me a halfwit!" he said, beginning to laugh himself.

When Hafner got himself a little under control, he gasped, "And the best part is, even if he complained, the grand jury would return a no-bill. Every member would be a lutefisk eater and unable to understand what the problem was!" He leaned back and said to Fields, "What about it? Next time you come to town, we'll treat you to an even better dinner. Have you ever tasted mutton with cabbage?"

"Or *gammelost?*" added Draxten.

"*Gammelost,*" breathed Nygaard reverently. "Boy, I wish we had some *gammelost.*"

Hafner said to Fields, "*gammelost* means cottage cheese, old, old, old cottage cheese. You keep it in a jar until it turns grey, and serve it up on bread and butter."

"It's wonderful," said Nygaard, who didn't disagree with Hafner's recipe for this treat, either. He caught the look on Fields' face and grinned. In a mock Norwegian accent he said, "Py Gott, Larry!" He nudged him, nearly knocking him off his chair. "Ve giff you some *gammelost* next time we see you, yah, shure!"

But in his eye was the savage anticipatory glint of a Viking whose hospitality had been insulted, and Fields, who had been savoring thoughts of a vengeful return match some time down the road, decided maybe he'd give Minnesota a complete miss next time. He looked down at the remains of his prune compote, nestled against a lump of lutefisk. "*Uff da,*" he said sadly.

.

NIGHT LIGHT

It started when a large object — circular, outlined with eerie lights — travelled with stately slowness across the evening Minnesota sky. It moved too slowly for an aircraft, and it made only a whisper of sound, as if powered by the ghost of a motor. Someone noticed that it was moving against the wind. Then, even as switchboards at the police and fire departments lit up like the Fourth of July all over again, it was gone. It made page two in next morning's *Hedeby Herald*.

Two nights later, Thursday, a farmer reported that something had gotten among his beef cattle in their nighttime pasture and killed two of them, leaving them in a boggy mire that had not been there the day before — and it had not rained in Hedeby County for over a month. The head of one had been neatly removed, and the other had been deprived of a leg. There were palm-size circles of singe scattered over both animals. The vet said it looked like they'd been electrocuted.

Whoever — whatever — did it had left no traces in the mud. This time the local TV news reporter did a feature on it, and the Minneapolis Star and Tribune phoned to inquire. The story was picked up by the wire services, but received little play.

Monday morning, a big old-fashioned "woody" station wagon slid to a halt in front of the Hedeby police station, and some half dozen Boy Scouts in the traditional khaki shorts and mosquito-bit knees piled out behind the traditional plump Scout Master, faces filled with less-traditional terror. They ran into the station, confronted the desk sergeant and began telling what had brought them in in such a mad rush.

". . . scared all night by . . ."

". . . big blue lights and . . ."

". . . loud noises . . ."

". . . smashed his cabin . . ."

". . . dead body!"

But being taken to the upstairs of a police station is a settling experience, even when the station is small and friendly as Hedeby's was. Something in the stolid patience of the cop bringing up the rear told them they had crossed unwarned that sudden line between freedom and custody. By the time they reached the two desks shoved head to head in the middle of the small squad room, man and boys had been reduced to silence.

Det. Sgt. Thor Nygaard turned toward them from the nearer desk. He was a very large man with football shoulders, pale blond hair and a Joe Palooka jaw. A half-empty coffee mug was almost entirely hidden in one massive paw. His cool blue eyes were steady on them while the cop explained their presence.

Sgt. Jack Hafner, at the farther desk, also studied this disruption to his morning. He was smaller only by comparison, darker, trimly built, with sea-gray eyes even cooler than his partner's. The Scouts shuffled uncomfortably.

"Uh, we, uh, want to report a murder," said the leader. "I think."

"Think, Wendal?" said Hafner. Hedeby was a city by grace of its charter, but in fact a small town. All its city officials knew one another by first name. Wendal Fridlund was County Clerk as well as Scoutmaster.

"It was a flying saucer," offered the littlest Scout, plump as Wendal, whom he resembled in facial features as well.

"Now, Henry, we don't know that — " began Wendal.

"Yeah, but something really spooky was going on across the lake, that's for sure," said another Scout, setting off a chorus of corroborative detail.

"How about we let Mr. Fridlund tell us what happened," suggested Nygaard, slicing firmly into the babble and silencing it. "Sit down, Wendal; you look all in." The big detective gestured at a hard wooden chair parked crossways to the end of his desk.

"Well, I am tired, Thor; I didn't sleep a wink last night," admitted the Scoutmaster, sinking down with a sigh.

"You want to tell us about it, Wendal?" said Hafner, getting up and coming around so he, too, could watch the scoutmaster's face.

"We'd been sitting around the campfire making s'mores and telling ghost stories — though we never got to the point where anyone was really scared, or anything; they're all too big to be scared by that stuff any more." Fridlund scratched absently at a dimpled knee. "It was eleven — time to shut down for the night — so I sent Henry and Nels to the lake with buckets. The rest of us began spading dirt onto the campfire. They brought the water and poured it over the dirt while I stirred, and the hissing was just starting to quit when we heard this scream." Wendal's pink face puckered up and the boys made uncomfortable sounds in the background. "I never in my entire life heard a scream like that, and I was in combat in Korea. It made the hair on my arms stand up. We all just froze, listening, but it didn't happen again. It was awful quiet for awhile; even the frogs and crickets shut up after that scream."

"There was just the one scream," said Hafner.

"Uh-huh, then this other noise started. It was a weird sound, I never heard one like it before. I can't describe it." One of the boys began emitting a high-pitched wheedle with a lot of air in it and the others nodded and pointed to him.

"Yes, it was just like that. Thank you, Gerald," said Wendal, and Gerald subsided, blushing with importance. "Not really loud, but you know how sound can carry across water. It was coming from across the lake, the same direction the scream came from. That's all private land over there, you know; Camp Nokomis has only half the lake. We hadn't seen a bit of activity over there — this being the weekend after Labor Day, everyone's pretty much closed up their cottages. But now, Sunday night, this terrible scream and odd noise.

"We grabbed a couple of lanterns and started for the beach to take a better look. There was a light on in one of the cabins, about where we were hearing the noise from. Then this real bright blue light just filled the trees over there like with a blue mist, and beams of it seemed to be coming down from the sky, and then sending fingers of it reaching across the lake right toward us." Wendal stopped to consider whether that might be a bit florid, decided it was accurate, and ran a downward- pointed finger across his forehead in a sweat-removing gesture.

"Now, I'm no coward." The cops nodded; Wendal had once faced down a bull that had cornered Henry in a pasture, and only last year dropped a garbage drum over a rabid skunk that had wandered into the Scout campground.

Wendal continued, "I grabbed the two nearest boys, hollered at the rest to follow me, and we all ran into my tent and zipped her shut. We felt around in the dark and found two of the hatchets, a bowie knife, Henry's Swiss army knife and two barbeque forks. I'm proud of my boys; they were scared, but they were ready to stand and fight if something tried to get into that tent."

Nygaard glanced around at the boys, who were all trying to look as if that were true.

"But whatever it was stayed on its own side of the lake," continued Wendal. "There were more noises, like tree branches breaking, big ones. Hooting, like giant owls. Groans. Hisses. And a big, ripping crash." His eye was caught by Nygaard's. "I am not exaggerating, and it seemed to go on for hours. We could sometimes see that light shining right through the tent, big and bright, like it was about to cross that lake and do unto us. Then the noise kind of faded away and stopped; and when we looked out, it was all dark there. But we stayed in that tent until daybreak, just in case."

"And because of that scream, you decided to come here and report a murder-you-think?" said Hafner.

"No. You see, Nels had told a story about a house where every so often there's a noise like a piano falling downstairs, only when they check, there isn't even a speck of dust out of place. Laugh if you like − " Indeed, Nygaard's blond head was back and his great Haw, haw, haw was filling the room − "But I wasn't going to come in with a report of all this and have you go out and find nothing. We hiked out to the parking lot and drove around the lake. It wasn't hard to find. Ollie Andersen's place − what's left of it.

"His cabin looks like some giant foot stepped on it. Roof all caved in and a wall down. There's trees snapped off and busted up all over the ground. There's a stink − " Again Wendal stopped, this time to wrinkle his nose. "An animal stink, like a zoo that needs its cages cleaned. And in the middle of all this was Ollie." One of the boys made a sound like a sob, and Wendel wiped his forehead with a forefinger again. "If a ghost or a thing from outer space kills someone, is it murder? We didn't come too close, but Ollie's deader'n anyone laying out just overnight should be."

Oliver Andersen was in fact very dead. The Medical Examiner, bent over the body, kept making a face very much like the one Wendal had made in describing it. The body was swollen and discolored. An arm appeared to have been dissected, and there were other unpleasantnesses. It was sprinkled with a yellowish powder and there was a cathouse stink about it that had spread to the leafy mould it lay on. When the ME at last had it loaded into a rubber bag and taken away, the cops sighed with relief and began their investigation.

Two good-size trees had been snapped off near their bases, and a number of smaller ones were shattered as well; the ground was covered with fresh bark and wood fragments.

All around the ruined cabin, the ground was thoroughly soaked. Hafner picked up something like a scrap of plastic trash bag, but thicker than any trash bag he had ever seen. The article was marked, its location noted and it was put away in case it was evidence.

An overnight bag found inside the ruined cabin indicated Andersen had had a guest. Tucked into a folded flannel shirt was a wallet.

"Victor Norbeck," said Hafner, looking at the driver's license. "What the devil was he doing out here?"

Because Norbeck and Andersen had once been partners in a waste disposal firm. There had been a serious quarrel over a $23,000 cash shortage, and each had publicly accused the other of theft. They dissolved the company and never spoke directly to one another again. Each had, however, spoken for the record to the press, and brought consequent suits for defamation on each other — thereby gaining the right to subpoena one another's private documents.

None of the documents had so far exposed the thief, but other pieces of dirty laundry kept coming to light and were dutifully put on public record. Ollie Andersen had been keeping a mistress in Minneapolis. Victor Norbeck had cheated on his income tax. Andersen had pornographic books and videotapes sent to a post office box he rented under an assumed name. Norbeck had made substantial campaign donations to both Republican and Democratic candidates for Tax Assessor. The citizens of Hedeby were delightfully scandalized by it all.

Both men knew they could no longer make a living in Hedeby — the Andersen cabin and Norbeck condo were for sale — because while the town was laughing at both of them, it was also disgusted with both of them. Andersen's wife had kicked him out of their house (which was why he was living in the cabin) and Norbeck's sister said she was sorry, but she felt he would be a bad influence on her children and he'd better not visit them any more.

So what had they been doing together? Maybe, mused Hafner, their mutual problems had finally brought the two to their senses, and they had met to work things out.

Only where was Norbeck?

On the other side of the ruined cabin there was a large oval of scorched, dead grass. "Sloppy pilot," muttered one of the cops.

"What's that, Tommy?" asked Nygaard.

Tommy pointed, "See, the flying saucer missed on its first pass and squashed the cabin. Then it landed here, alongside."

"Flying saucer?" drawled Hafner, and Nygaard turned away with a heavy sigh.

Embarrassed, the cop doggedly added, "No, I'm serious; this has the earmarks of a close encounter. If the news stories are right, if a spacecraft landed here, the burnt place should be radioactive."

"You been reading too many National Enquirers," said Nygaard. But a cop near the center of the oval decided he'd scuffled the black dust thoroughly enough, and walked with what he hoped would pass as a casual pace out of it. Two others who had been standing on the edge of the oval backed up.

"Now see what you started?" demanded Nygaard. "How can we conduct an investigation if everybody's all spooked about flying saucers?"

Tommy folded his arms and said, "I'm only saying you should keep an open mind. A thousand people saw that UFO the other night, and it wasn't a lost wolf from the iron range that killed two of Mr. Hagedorn's beef cattle. And where's Victor Norbeck?"

"Wherever he is, it isn't in a flying saucer!" said Hafner, his sea-gray eyes growing stormy.

Nygaard said, "Maybe we can stop this nonsense right now." The big man went out on the road where the Police Reserve van was parked. The van dated from the old days, when the Reserves were called Civil Defense; the old emblem could still be traced under the new paint on the door. Nygaard looked in the back, and sure enough, the old geiger counter case was still there. The case had been spot welded to the floor, and no one had thought to remove the counter and put something else in the case. The batteries were dead, but the reservist loaned them some from his flashlight, and Nygaard carried the clicking device back to the scene. As he approached, the clicks came closer together, then when he held the geiger counter down to the spot, the clicks came so fast they were a buzz.

"See?" said Tommy, vindicated. "See? I told you!"

A thorough search for Victor Nybeck was performed, spreading in later hours from the Anderson property onto neighboring properties and into the lake. But no trace was found.

Andersen's body was a shock, but Norbek's disappearance was spooky. There was no sign that something violent had happened to a second body anywhere on the scene, Yet Norbeck was not at home, and no one had seen him for at least twenty-four hours. His big-tired pickup was not in its slot behind the apartment building. They found evidence that a fat-tired vehicle with a large wheelbase had pulled in beside Andersen's car at the cabin. It wasn't there now, though Andersen's Cordova was.

The Cordova, though its battery was fully charged, would not start, would not even turn over; nor would its headlights or other electrical systems work. By Sunday afternoon the news people from as far away as Chicago were asking about satellite uplinks at Hedeby's little television station.

Early Tuesday morning, a big dusty pickup pulled wearily into a gas station outside of Hedeby. Harold Nilsson, owner/ operator, barely awake, came out to see what this early-bird wanted, and found a man sitting behind the wheel in a dazed condition.

"Fill it up for you?" asked Nilsson.

"Fill − " The man's head came slowly around. "I'm empty," he agreed. "Hungry," he amended.

"Hey, you all right, mister?"

"Where am I?"

"Highway 49 and County Road DD. Where you headed?"

"I'd like to go home, now, please."

"Where's that?"

The man frowned, then shook his head. "I'm sorry."

"Well, what's your name?"

"I think . . ." He shrugged, looked at Nilsson with scared eyes. "They called me . . . Earthman."

"I think you better not drive any more right now, okay?"

The man looked at his hands gripping the steering wheel. "No more driving," he said, relieved, and relaxed the hands until they slid off the wheel. Then he stumbled out of the truck and went into the station. Nilsson trailed a wary distance behind him, watched the man study the pay phone on the wall a thought-gathering while, then reach into his pocket and pull out, not coins, but a fistful of the same yellowish dust that covered his pickup. He sifted this onto the floor, sat down beside it and began to cry.

An ambulance took Norbeck — for he was in fact the missing man — to St. Mary's in Hedeby, where he was pronounced exhausted and in shock. He was admitted, put to bed and went immediately to sleep. A few hours later the county extension agent announced that the mysterious powder that had filled Norbeck's pockets, dusted his truck and sifted across Anderson's body was lycopodium, the spores of mushrooms.

A small crowd gathered in the hall outside Norbeck's hospital room: four daily newspaper reporters, two radio announcers, and a woman who claimed she was a stringer for the National Star. There was even a TV camera crew from a network news program. Other patients well enough to take an interest were all agog at the lights and talk, and several of the nurses were interviewed by newshounds with impatient editors.

Hafner wanted to lay legal hands on Norbeck, bring him to the squad room and ask him pointed questions. But the police hadn't been notified that Norbeck had been found until after he'd been admitted, and by the time the two detectives got to the hospital, Norbeck was safe asleep and the corridor outside his room was a circus of impatient, cynical and nosy reporters.

Thor Nygaard took up a position at Norbeck's bedside. He was the larger of the two, better able to handle any hysterics from the man, or opportunistic maneuvers on the part of the press. Jack Hafner went off to continue investigating what one reporter, looking into the camera with pontifical solemnity, named the "best-documented close encounter of the decade." The Chief called it "that damned Anderson murder."

Hafner dug up records, asked questions, and in fairly short order found himself in the company of a professor from the University, Dr. John Christianson, who had something he called a gamma spectrometer. It sat in the back of his van, tied down: a large, round, cold thing that breathed vapor when disturbed. Cables snaked everywhere, connecting enough boxes of assorted colors to make an electronics wizard groan. Dr. Christianson wanted to examine the radioactive scorch mark.

"Studying the radiation could tell us a lot about the power source of this flying saucer." His blue eyes twinkled. "Or it may prove a defect in your geiger counter. And it will be a nice field test of the portable spectrometer." Which was the real reason he'd come down from the Twin Cities, probably. Dr. Christianson was an enthusiast, a believer in testing field equipment under field conditions. A tall, thin man, his hair had once been fiery red. The red had faded to blond and gray, but the freckles remained. They drove to the ruined cabin and Christianson got out to see what the bumpy ride might have done to his equipment. But it was built well and nothing was damaged. They scooped up a sample of the scorched earth for the machine, and soon a spiky green line was growing across the computer display.

Freckled hands rattled across a keyboard; the display froze, then grew letters and numbers. "Interesting," Christianson grunted. "Americium-241."

"What's that?" Hafner asked.

"It's a transuranic — a synthetic element. Doesn't exist in nature; somebody has to make it."

"What's it used for?"

"On Earth? Smoke detectors."

"It's really strange," said Hafner over the phone to Nygaard. "We can't make Americium without making a whole lot of other elements at the same time, the professor says. Kind of like cracking oil to get naphtha. What did they do with the rest of the stuff? And why use naphtha for fuel? Gasoline's better."

"Please, Jack," Nygaard begged. "Don't catch any flying saucers. I'm trapped here between the reporters and their prey; and they've been trying all afternoon to get an official admission from me that a flying saucer did all this. Prove Norbeck did it. Prove *I* did it. But please don't prove little green men from outer space did it!"

The newspaper and TV people had all gone off in search of dinner. Nygaard persuaded a nurse to bring him a pot of coffee — a single cup was never enough — but he was only halfway through his second cup when Chief Thorpe called. "What the hell are you two up to?" he demanded.

"We're investigating the Anderson murder," said Nygaard, who could be very literal.

"Yeah, but you been driving Stark in the lab nuts. Test this for PCBs, how do you set magnesium on fire, how many pounds of pull to break a seven-inch aspen off at the base? And Hafner just drove by here with Joe Swenson and his bloodhound. I repeat, what are you two up to?"

"Chief, do you believe in flying saucers?"

Thorpe hung up, and Nygaard was left in peace for an hour.

The news people got back from dinner, to find Norbeck awake. Thor Nygaard watched from the door, no longer the center of attention, while Norbeck himself held audience inside.

"I remember most of it, but there's chunks missing," he said. "A lot of it was like a dream. I was visiting Ollie at his cabin. He'd invited me out to see if we couldn't find a way to put an end to our feud. I remember arriving, but then there's a blank. Something happened, something noisy I think, then I woke up in this big white room strapped to a table like an operating table, and there were these little pale guys in green robes looking at me. No noses, and no ears. No hair or eyelashes. Pale skin, the color of — of mushrooms. Real long fingers, skinny and delicate. No fingernails. One of 'em had a little, bitty box he wore hanging around his neck, and a kind of squeaky voice came out of it whenever he wanted to talk to me. I never saw 'em talk to each other.

"They took me out of that room to another room. They had my truck there; they put me in the truck and told me to start it, and drive. They had some kind of trick camera that made scenes in front of the windshield; and I must've drove over every kind of terrain in the universe, hours and hours, while they stood around and watched. The scenes were three-D, and when I'd run over something the truck would jump. And when I'd crash, it would hurt, only then I'd be all right and it would start in again. They wouldn't let me stop. Man, the first thing I'm gonna do when I get out of here is sell that truck. I don't ever want my backside to rest on that seat again!"

The phone rang. It was Jack Hafner, and Nygaard could hear the grin in his voice. "We got him."

"Who?"

"The little green man. Or he will be, in just a few minutes." Hafner explained the progress of the investigation, concluding, "Is he awake?"

Nygaard looked at Norbeck who was obliging the reporters by making a sketch of the alien and his squeaky box. "Yep."

"Good. Watch him close; I'll be there in five minutes."

Hafner was as good as his word, Norbeck was describing the control cabin of the saucer when he was interrupted by a strange noise outside his window. It was a high, whistling, warbling noise, very much like the sound Gerald the Boy Scout had made in the upstairs squad room.

Norbeck ignored the sound for a few seconds, then turned toward it as if annoyed – then started violently. He threw the covers off the bed and leaped to the floor, shoving reporters out of the way. "It's them!" he shouted. "They've come to take me back!"

Large hands landed on Norbeck's shoulders and he looked up into a calm, pleasant face under a sheaf of blond hair. "Take it easy,

Victor," said Nygaard. "The only people after you are us. You are under arrest for the malicious killing of cattle, for destruction of property and for the murder of Oliver Anderson. You have a right to remain silent. If you give up the right to remain silent, you have a right to consult with an attorney before questioning, and to have an attorney present during questioning. Do you understand these rights as I have explained them to you?"

Norbeck had been backing up during all of this, back to his bed, onto the bed. He tucked his feet under the sheet and coverlet. "No," he said.

"No, what?" asked Nygaard.

"It was those little men, the men with mushroom faces."

"Lay off him, okay?" said the woman reporter. "Can't you see he's scared half to death?"

But one of the other reporters had gone to the window to look out. "Commere, Joey; get a shot of this!" he said, gesturing at the man with the TV camera on his shoulder. "Look, over there!" There was a rush of reporters to the window, but Norbeck didn't even look in that direction.

"What is it?" asked the cameraman, trying to push through the crowd, then, "Aw, it's nothing but a pickup truck!"

A reporter said, "Yeah, but what's that on top of the exhaust pipe? See? Sticking up beside the cab?"

Another reporter said, "I dunno, but it's what's making that weird noise; see how those people are trying to make the driver shut his engine off?"

"Why don't you go down and ask?" suggested Nygaard. "No telling what else the driver of that truck can tell you about our investigation."

Which wouldn't be much, but it cleared the room. "It's a calliope whistle, right, Victor?" said Nygaard to Norbeck when they were gone. "To disguise the sound of an engine under stress. If I wanted to use my bumper winch to pull down a couple trees, someone hearing it might be able to tell what was happening unless I disguised the sound. It'd work just as well for the generator on back, in case I felt like electrocuting a cow or two, or maybe a business partner."

They'd taken Norbeck off to the police station, for booking, and the reporters had scattered like the construction crew at the Tower of Babel. Hafner and Nygaard spent a couple of hours questioning Norbeck, then taking down his statement which would be presented with other evidence to the County Prosecutor. Then they went to unwind at the Uff-Da Inn. They were not surprised to find Don Olavsen, reporter for the *Hedeby Herald*, already waiting at their usual table.

"You look pleased with yourself, Jack," Olavsen said. "Sit down. Relax. Have a beer." He snagged the passing waitress. "And then, perhaps, you can tell the local press a bit more than the pitiful few nuggets you gave the out-of-towners. Or do I have to wait until Norbeck's book comes out?" He looked at the two surprised faces of his friends. "Didn't you hear? He's looking for an agent."

Hafner made a disgusted sound. He waited until his Schell's came, then again while he savored its flavor. "You know we can't spill our case before the trial." He took another, deeper drink. "But I must admit, this one's a stinker. And it would be nice to have somebody get it all-the-way right for once, not just rework what's left after the lawyers get through. Promise not to let things out until they've been brought up in court? But that you'll break the story in time to spoil any book deal Norbeck might be making?"

Olavsen crossed his heart and hoped to die. And since he'd always kept that particular oath, they told him.

"We figured from the start it was Norbeck," Nygaard began, "because he was the one with the motive. He stole the $23,000 from the disposal firm, and Anderson finally found out about it. He told his lawyer about it, and though the proof itself is still missing, the lawyer will be able to testify about that conversation.

Hafner continued, "The problem wasn't lack of evidence – there was evidence all over the place: the shattered trees, the squashed cabin, the strip of plastic, the yellow powder, the animal stink, the mud. The problem was finding an explanation for it, sifting the important out of the unimportant, and linking it all to Norbeck. That might have proved difficult. Norbeck was a professional disposer, if not a very honest one. He and Anderson were being sued for illegal dumping in half a dozen places, from the days when they were a disposal company. Didn't the Herald kick off that investigation?

"A former employee tipped us off," nodded Olavsen. "Said they were so sloppy it scared him into quitting."

"Sloppy is right," said Hafner. "Joe Swenson's bloodhound found a trail of that stink from where Anderson's body was found to the place where the truck was parked, and again on a pair of trousers at a disposal site — along with a lot of other interesting items."

"Anderson's trousers?" asked Olavsen.

"Norbeck's, by the look of them," said Hafner. "We found out from their records where they'd been burying stuff, and took the bloodhound around to them. Third place we tried, he bayed and pawed the ground, so we dug and found all sorts of stuff.

"Dr. Christianson's spectrometer found Americium 241 at the site of the murder, and in Norbeck's old workshop. It was on the same trousers the hound dug up, too.

"There was a big glass beaker, radioactive as all get-out, with traces of acid in the bottom. And there were lots of smoke detectors, old ones, with the innards ripped apart. Open up your own smoke detector: that little metal box is radioactive. Americium-241, just like the mark out at Anderson's cabin. Dissolve a couple dozen of those boxes in acid and slosh it over the grass, and you'll get a radioactive scorch mark, all right! The stink? That was a half empty bottle of the stuff deer hunters pour on their boots to keep the deer from smelling them. Disgusting stuff; I'd sooner let a deer get away from me than have that pong hanging around me all day.

"And then we found an Ag Bag, one of those things the farmers use for storage when the silo or granary is full. It was in two pieces, and one of them was heat sealed around a hose. It had burst, and the bit of plastic we found at the cabin fits into the tear. What you want to bet the water still in it analyzes as coming from Anderson's well-pump?"

Nygaard was grinning at Olavsen. "Don't you see? Figure that sealed-up bag was twelve square. Put it that up on a roof, empty, and hook the hose to a pump, and it'll weigh over ten tons before it's full. Enough to squash a cabin, easy."

Hafner sipped his beer and continued, "The fusible links on Anderson's car were blown – easy to do, hard to find. And we found a boom box with a cassette tape still in it. Careless and sloppy. Because we played that tape, after fingerprinting it, and found it was a selection of sound effects. Guess who's fingerprints were on it?

"There was a batch of magnesium curls – somebody must have been machining the stuff – and they would burn with a nice blue-white light. A bit of mist on the lake, the shadows of trees: there are your fingers of light reaching towards the scout camp.

"People throw the damndest things away – and Norbeck was the hazardous waste man for the whole county. At this point, it looks like almost everything that happened at Oliver Anderson's cabin can be explained by the contents of that dump."

"The only thing we can't figure out," said Nygaard, "is the thing that started this off. That flying saucer everyone saw about a week ago."

At this, Don set down his beer and raised his index finger. "Never underestimate the power of the press," he declaimed. "That one is the lead story on tomorrow's 'Lifestyles' page."

Nygaard leaned well into Olavsen's space. "Give," he said.

"It's the flying club, out at the airport. They've been practicing flying in formation for an air show. They were out late one evening with their landing lights on, and the ground watcher said it looked like a flying saucer had buzzed the field. Your mind fills in the blanks: get a bunch of lights in a circle, against a dark background, all moving in unison – next thing you know, people are reporting a circular object outlined with lights. At anything over five or six thousand feet you barely hear the engines. They've been making jokes about how everyone thinks they've been buzzed by a saucer. The club cafe even has a 'saucer plate' for $3.95 – 'unidentified frying objects'."

Nygaard began to laugh his great Haw, haw, haw. "That's what gave Norbeck the idea!" he said, still laughing.

"The jerk," agreed Hafner, more soberly, seeing the mutilated body of Oliver Anderson with his mind's eye. There had been a lot of hatred between the two, but nothing could justify what Norbeck had done to his former partner.

"But what set you off so hard after him?" asked Olavsen. "I mean, didn't you even think for a minute it could really be a close encounter?"

"The close encounter happened when Norbeck cranked up that generator, dropped a chain off the back of his truck for a ground, then went and honked at Ollie to come out and lay hands on the truck. That was the scream Wendel heard: Ollie dying by electrocution."

"It's simple, Don," said Nygaard. "Norbeck was dumb enough to give us just two choices: him or flying saucers. And he did a good job, making it look like a saucer.

"But neither Jack nor me believes in flying saucers."

TIMELY PSYCHIATRIC INTERVENTION

"No, no, it's not that he's gone right 'round the bend," said Natterly. "He's mostly sort of like he's always been. Only more so."

Dr. Bach nodded and tried to look understanding. The problem with these superheated brains, he thought, is that they don't really know what normal is any more. Why he'd agreed to be the house psychiatrist to the inmates of a think tank he'd never know. That wasn't true, of course. The reason was money. After years of untenured teaching, he'd leaped at this offer like a hungry bass after a pickerel frog. "Tell me," he said, "just what appears to be the problem?"

Natterly was Joe McCain's supervisor, a very tall, thin man with indoor skin. He shrugged. "Well, he's working on something very − sensitive. And he's touchy about it, but he smiles a lot. And you know McCain, he never smiles."

Dr. Bach didn't know McCain, not very well. He remembered him as a sour-mouthed, taciturn little man with dark eyes that darted everywhere. Macbeth, about Act IV. Bach gave the psychiatrist's standard reply. "Go on."

"Oh, he's always been a little strange − " Natterly gave a nervous laugh and tucked his handkerchief deeper into his shirt pocket, his inevitable sign of distress. "Always thinking people are plotting to take credit for his work, or something. He types his own reports, you know. Won't allow a secretary near his notes. He's just as sure one of us would love to take a look at his pet project as he ever was, but now he smiles when he lets on he thinks so. And it's not a nice smile."

Though he thought that rather thin, Bach agreed to have McCain in for a talk. An appointment was set up for late the next afternoon — for all the jokes, a mad scientist is not a healthy thing to have in a high-tech research lab — and McCain proved himself prompt.

He strode in on the dot, glanced around the comfortable office, shied visibly at the stuffed owl on a shelf, and sat down. He was in gray slacks, cream shirt and green tweed sport coat, his going-home clothes. "All right, I'm here!" he announced, and studied Dr. Bach from under a massive dome of forehead with uncommonly keen blue eyes.

There was an uncomfortable silence, then McCain abruptly relaxed and said, "Please forgive me. I've always been a suspicious man, seeing conspiracies everywhere. When Natterly told me I was to come and see you, it threw me because he wasn't the least bit subtle about it. I'm used to subtleties; overt actions confuse me." He smiled, an honest smile, and that simple action transformed him into a charming elf.

"Natterly tells me you are being unusually close-mouthed about your latest project."

McCain's eyebrows raised. "I have to be! Good heavens, man, I've only reported a quarter of what I've discovered, and they've slapped a Top Secret label on that!"

"But as your supervisor, surely Natterly is on the list, however short, of those who need to know."

McCain's back curved a little, and his head pulled back into his shoulders. The elf was gone, replaced by a paranoid gnome. "He knows all he needs to know."

"Well, can you tell me about it?"

"You?!"

"In order to perform my job, I've been given the highest possible clearances, and I am to be given access to anything I judge to be important to the care of my patients. And I never, ever speak of such matters outside the confines of this office."

"So I'm a patient, am I?" The look was becoming malignant.

"Everyone who works here is my patient," Dr. Bach said, keeping it light, waving his hand to indicate the depth and breadth of his load.

The malignancy retreated, a little. "So, what do you want to know?"

"First, what is it you're working on?"

"Time travel." He said it so off-handedly that it took a few seconds to sink in.

"Time travel?" Bach had been hearing rumors for months, but --

"Certainly. I've built a prototype machine and I've been doing some experiments, on rats, mostly." He looked up at Dr. Bach from under that forehead and smiled a mischievous elf- smile. "Oh, I'm aware of the paradoxes. The most serious one is proving anything has happened. For example, if I were to travel back to this morning and change this sport coat for my navy blue blazer, then I would have walked in here wearing it and I'd never convince you I ever came in wearing the sport coat. See? I go back and make a change and since the moment then arrives in its new form, how does anyone know it's changed? Would even I remember? Very interesting."

"You're saying it's possible for you to do that? Go back and change something?"

"Of course. In fact, I plan on doing that first thing in the morning. I'm going to kill my father."

Dr. Bach gaped, then grinned. "But think of the paradoxes! If you kill your father, then you would never be born. And if you are never born, then you don't invent a time machine. And if you don't invent a time machine then your father will live, so you will be born, so — "

McCain laughed. "Don't be an idiot! I intend to kill my father only after I am conceived. My father was a cruel, hard, unpleasant man, a drunk. We lived in the worst apartment in the worst part of town. He blamed me for the death of his wife — she died right after I was born — and he made my life hell. He's going to die, so I can have a better upbringing. And it'll look like an accident; because I don't want an innocent person accused of it. And, anyway, I think it would be small improvement to be the orphan child of a murdered man.

"It's likely my grandfather will raise me: he had a farm, and that is a far healthier environment for a child than a slum." Again the keen glance. "You think I don't know what I am? You think you're the first psychiatrist who has tried to help? Bah! I know what would help, and I'm going to go do it!"

This was an entirely new approach to an old problem, and Dr. Bach said he would be interested in seeing the result. McCain promised to come in again the next day.

He strode in on the dot, glanced around the comfortable office, shied visibly at the stuffed owl on a shelf, and sat down. He was in gray slacks, blue shirt and navy blue blazer, his going-home clothes. "All right, I'm here!" he announced, and studied Dr. Bach from under a massive dome of forehead with uncommonly keen blue eyes.

There was an uncomfortable silence, then McCain abruptly relaxed and said, "Please forgive me. I've always been a suspicious man, seeing conspiracies everywhere. When Natterly told me I was to come and see you, it threw me because he wasn't the least bit subtle about it. I'm used to subtleties; overt actions confuse me." If he'd smiled, Dr. Bach might have found him more human.

"Natterly tells me you are being unusually close-mouthed about your latest project," said Dr. Bach. "May I ask what it is you're working on? It's all right to tell me: I have the highest possible clearances, and I never talk shop with anyone."

"Time travel." He said it so off-handedly that it took a few seconds to sink in.

"TIME travel?"

"Certainly. I've built a prototype machine and I've been doing some experiments." He looked up at Dr. Bach from under that forehead. "Oh, I'm aware of the paradoxes, and that the most serious one is proving anything has happened. But I plan on trying it anyway, first thing in the morning. I'm going to kill my grandfather. He raised me when my father died in a car accident shortly after the death of my mother."

McCain gaped, then grinned. "But think of the paradoxes! If you kill your grandfather, then your father would never be born, and then you would never be conceived. And if there's no you, then there's no time machine. And if you don't invent a time machine then your grandfather will live, so you will be born, so − "

"Don't be an idiot!" McCain barked. "I intend to kill my grandfather only after my father is conceived. The death of my parents was a terrible blow to my development. If they had lived, I'd have grown up in the city, with its libraries and other children to play with. My grandfather was a cruel, hard, unpleasant man, suspicious and miserly. He kept me strictly confined to that shambles he called a farm. My environment was so deprived that I'm sure that's the reason I grew up to be so − strange." Again the keen glance. "You think I don't know what I am? You think you're the first psychiatrist who has tried to help? Bah! I know what would help, and I'm going to go do it!"

He promised to come see Dr. Bach the next day and let him know what had happened.

He strode in on the dot, glanced around the comfortable office, shied visibly at the stuffed owl on a shelf, and sat down. He was in dark brown slacks, cream shirt and tan sport coat, his going-home clothes. "All right, I'm here!" he announced, studying Dr. Bach from under a massive dome of forehead with uncommonly keen blue eyes.

There was an uncomfortable silence, then McCain abruptly relaxed and said, "Forgive me. I've always been a suspicious man, seeing conspiracies everywhere. I don't know how Natterly is going to run a proper conspiracy, coming right out and telling me to visit you; and he'd better hope I don't figure it out. Maybe he's realized overt actions confuse me."

"Natterly tells me you're being unusually close-mouthed about your latest project. May I ask what you are working on?"

"Time travel."

"TIME travel?"

"Certainly. I've built a prototype machine and I've been doing some experiments, on rats, mostly." He scowled up at Dr. Bach from under that forehead. "Oh, I'm aware of the paradoxes, but I plan on trying it first thing in the morning, anyway. I'm going to kill my uncle. As my only living relative, he raised me. It would have been better if he had never been born. He was a cruel, hard, unpleasant man, suspicious and miserly. He put me to work at an early age and never let me keep a dime of what I earned. Paper routes, lawn mowing, snow shoveling, then soda jerking. I worked my way through high school and worked in college to buy clothes and pay rent — scholarships don't cover everything, you know. I never learned to play, never learned how to establish a relationship with anyone. That's a pity: a man of my intelligence should have children, pass along those genes. So I'm going to go back and kill him."

Dr. Bach felt a vague unease at the thought of a whole family of little McCain's. He extracted a promise from the scientist that he come in again the next day and let him know what had happened.

"It was that terrible orphanage I was raised in!" he shouted. "No normal loving relationship with my own people. They all started dying right about the time I was born. It was almost as if there were some kind of plot to destroy me!"

"Settle down," Dr. Bach said soothingly, reaching for the secret button under the edge of his desk. But McCain made a serious effort to calm himself, and Bach brought his hand back to the desk's shining surface. Possibly McCain was right: being raised by blood relatives, even less-than-perfect ones, might have made an enormous difference to this man. Meanwhile, better distract him with a less-explosive subject. "Could we explore for a moment your obvious reaction to my stuffed owl?"

"Humph!" snorted McCain. "I'm allergic to feathers."

Disappointed, Dr. Bach tried another subject. "Will you tell me what project it is you're working on? I assure you I have the highest clearances, and I never talk shop."

"I don't care what your clearance is, I won't tell you about it. I won't tell anyone about it until I've tried it out and discover that it works."

"When do you think that might be?"

"I don't know. But it's just a matter of time." A malignant smile flickered briefly.

"Can't you give me a better estimate than that? I assure you, this may be very pertinent."

"I don't care how pertinent you think it is, I don't think it's pertinent at all, and I won't tell you." There was an uncomfortable, thought-filled silence, then McCain said, almost to himself, "A man with your clearances should have other ways of finding out what I'm working on."

That was exactly what Dr. Bach was thinking, and his face betrayed him.

"I tell you what," said McCain, the smile now very ugly indeed. "I'm going to try out that machine first thing tomorrow morning. If it works, you'll be the first to know."

A SPECIALIST IN DRAGONS

It was a bright and beautiful morning, though it promised to be hot by afternoon. Baron Halfdan of Thorney was riding the fields on his destrier, visiting the peasants and checking on the crops. His pretty daughter Halla rode beside on her brown mare, keeping him company. Since they were well within his lands, they had dispensed with the usual rattling company of retainers; they were alone together.

There was a sudden leathery flapping, and an enormous blue dragon alighted on the lane in front of them. Before Halfdan could react, the dragon snatched Halla out of her saddle with one large foreclaw. She screamed and kicked violently, but it ignored her. "You're Halfdan?" it hissed smokily.

"Yea! Release the girl, lizard!" roared Halfdan, drawing his sword and kicking his horse forward. He slashed at the dragon's claw, drawing purple blood in a great spurt that stained his beard and tunic, but the dragon ignored that, too. It leaned forward and bit the destrier's head off with a horrible neatness, then rose on its wings with a loud whap-whap-whap and disappeared over a copse of alders.

Halfdan untangled himself from the ruin of his stallion, cursing. He was a big man, with more black hair on his body than was really needful or attractive; and the blood dripping off the hem of his yellow tunic did not improve his appearance. He looked around and saw the terrified mare lunging against her reins, caught on a thorn bush a few dozen yards up the lane. He trotted up to her, calmed her and climbed awkwardly into the unfamiliar woman's saddle. It was indicative of his fury, anxiety, and need to find help quickly that he did so; but he cut across the fields rather than risk being seen riding a mare.

Halfdan hid her behind a neatly whitewashed cottage a few minutes later and came up the path to pound on the door. He glanced down at himself and hoped his gory appearance would not shock Wulfstan. But then, Wulfstan was a wizard, probably used to far more horrible sights than a blood-covered mortal.

Halfdan wanted two things: his daughter back, and his sword healed. Already the dragon's blood had begun to eat its way into the metal. Wiping at the blood served only to spread it further up the blade. Leg-Biter had been his father's sword, and his grandfather's. It was famous for holding its edge through the longest battles, and it was the most valuable weapon the baron owned. He impatiently hammered at the door. What was the use of buying a wizard if he wouldn't answer his door?

Halfdan boldly lifted the latch and went in. The wizard's raven screeched in alarm, and flew to the rafters with a great clattering of wings. "Here, here!" it croaked. "The wizard is out! Have you got an appointment? Take two cups of wine and call on him in the morning!"

"None of that, Hugin! Look at this sword! Dragon's blood, fresh from the dragon!" The baron waved the weapon in the general direction of the raven. "He stole Halla! Get your master, and get him fast!"

Hugin sneezed at the purple smell. He flew higher into the ceiling beams and crouched with his eyes shut.

"Hugin, I bought a very large cat at the fair last week," said Halfdan dangerously. "He's extremely fond of fowl."

"Yes? But my master's conjuring an elemental, and it will take a certain delicacy of approach."

"Delicacy be damned! Fetch him or I'll fetch my cat!"

The bird screamed, "All right, all right, all right!" He swooped down and out an open window. "Humans have no respect for a raven's feelings," he grumbled as he flew off.

The baron sat down and looked about. This was only the second time he'd visited Wulfstan's cottage since he'd acquired him last month. There were two rooms and a half loft. One room was a kitchen and the other, the bigger, was a clutter of shabby-comfortable furniture, books and paraphernalia Halfdan intended never to inquire too closely about. He briefly wondered where all the dust had come from; surely there was more than a month's worth?

He was studying a moth-eaten tapestry showing a wizard conjuring up a wind for a sea captain when Wulfstan came bustling in. "Sorry you had to wait, I was doing some lab work on the harvest weather. Your problem is dragons, Hugin said."

"Dragon, Wulfstan. I hope you can do something, and quickly." He displayed his sword, now badly corroded. "I wounded a dragon with this not an hour ago and look at it! And Halla — he took Halla away with him."

"Really?" Wulfstan produced a tablet and stylus from thin air. He was young yet, a very thin man with glowing dark eyes. His dirty blue wizard's gown had a smell of ozone about it and a peculiar pattern of holes burned into the sleeves. Despite the shabby robe — perhaps even because of it — he was the picture of wizardly dignity. "What kind of dragon, my lord? Any special characteristics?"

"It seemed a perfectly ordinary dragon, maybe a bit larger than usual. Blue and silver. Not like those oriental things."

Wulfstan was taking quick notes. "What about your daughter? Did she provoke him?"

The baron thought. Fifteen-year-old Halla had his own imperious temper, and was perfectly capable of provoking a dragon if it seemed the thing to do. "No, we didn't see it until it landed. And once he landed there wasn't time. He grabbed her and asked if I were Halfdan."

"Hmmm. So he was specifically after Halla. Uh — is she a virgin, by chance?"

The baron was taken aback. "Of course! I've warned the neighborhood bucks about her. Flaying alive for the first man who so much as kisses her. I'm saving her to marry to Baron Aethelwold." Halfdan combed his beard with his fingers, flinging bits of dried blood in all directions. "Decent sort, he'll treat her okay. But he'll die young of the apoplexy — all his line does — and she'll hold the land . . ." His eyes had gone dreamy, but he suddenly jerked back to the present. "Why? Is it that important?"

"Halfdan, either the dragon's got a taste for young female flesh, or some wizard sent him after a virgin for a spell he's working. Let's hope for the latter."

The baron looked stricken by simultaneous doses of hope and despair. Wulfstan lay down his tablet with a serious expression. "We'll have to call in a specialist on this."

"Specialist?"

"A specialist in dragons. I'm just a general wizard, fine with elementals, healing magicks, and weather. But dragons are a bit beyond me. Fortunately Marduk of Oxney is very good with dragons, and he lives nearby. He's expensive, but what specialist isn't? I'll call and check if he'll see us right away."

The wizard reached out and took a crystal into his hands. He gazed into it and his body stiffened, became outlined in a faint blue light. He stayed that way for quite a long time. Even a glowing wizard can be a boring sight after a while, if glow is all he does; Halfdan sighed and picked up a small silver knife to take a closer look at the runes incised on its blade.

"My lord," the wizard said irritably, "can't you control yourself around blades? Now I'll have to re-consecrate that athame before I can use it again." The baron started, looked guilty, and set the knife down. Wulfstan had stopped glowing and was once more aware of his surroundings.

"What did Marduk say?"

Wulfstan rose and began to strip off his robe, revealing tunic and hose beneath. "He wants us there as soon as possible. You go get us a pair of good horses, while I pack some equipment." He began rummaging in a box of old phials; dust rose about him. "Quickly, please!" he said. "Every minute counts."

Within half an hour they were riding down Oxney Road. Baron Halfdan held the stained sword across his pommel, carefully wrapped in virgin wool according to Wulfstan's instructions. As promised, the day had grown hot; and after galloping some distance, they had to pull back into a walk to cool the horses. Halfdan moodily commented that it would have been nice if this expensive specialist could have conjured them into his presence. "I hear there's a wizard over Stowold way who can do that."

"Aelfric of Stowold is a specialist in telekinesis," Wulfstan explained patiently. "He once moved an entire castle for his owner."

"Yes? Well, why didn't you call him? Couldn't he bring Halla back to me?"

Wulfstan smiled grimly. "Yes, my lord. But summoning live persons without harming them is prohibitively expensive. You could sell this barony without meeting his price. I think we'll have to be satisfied with Marduk. Anyway, I'm doing the best I can to smooth this ride. If you'll notice, there's a shower up ahead, wetting down the dust. And see that small white cloud travelling with us, keeping off the sun? If you weren't riding with me, you'd be choking and sweating."

"Yes, sorry. I guess I'm distracted by all this." They continued in silence, each wrapped in his own thoughts. Halfdan was a little surprised at the strength of his distress. After all, Halla was only a girl. She was strong, bright and witty, like her two brothers now being educated at Earl Edgar's castle. He'd saved Edgar's life in battle a few years ago, and this was Halfdan's price for the favor. The Earl had no sons and his daughters were exceptionally homely. He might have to settle for a baron's son for them.

With such bright prospects, surely Halla was not very important. So why was his heart so heavy? Perhaps because he had felt no great need to exploit her and had allowed himself to know her as a person. And she was a chip off the old block, all right. Poor Aethelwold would probably die years earlier than necessary unless he learned how to handle her. Halfdan smiled, then frowned. First, of course, they'd have to get her back.

Marduk's "cottage" was very nearly a small castle, with a crenellated wall and a high tower from which he could study the stars. To the left of the wall was a church with its graveyard, and to the right a forest; Marduk could gather his bats, toads and herbs readily. In front of the gate Marduk stood waiting, wearing a robe of Tyrian purple with runes of power embroidered in threads of all the seven metals − even quicksilver, which moved and shifted but stayed nonetheless in its pattern. His long hair was gold and silver, and a small owl was perched on his shoulder.

Marduk invited them in and treated them to fragrant cups of something which, while hot, was nevertheless very refreshing. "I think I can help you," he said to Halfdan. "But it will be expensive."

Halfdan's heart sank. "How much?"

"Five ounces of gold," Marduk said.

"And what do I get for my gold?"

"I'll find out what dragon has your daughter, whether she's alive, and what he intends to do with her. Then I'll be able to say more about what the rescue will involve."

Halfdan took five large coins from his purse, which Wulfstan had insisted he refill before they set out. He gave them to Marduk, who immediately led them to a large and very impressive hall. Two freshly-drawn pentacles were on the floor, linked by obscure signs in an ancient language. Marduk took the sword and balanced it upright on its point in the center of one pentacle; he stood the baron in the center of the other.

"Think of the dragon, every detail you can," the wizard said; then he froze Halfdan's thought with a quick stab of his wand. Facing the other pentacle, Marduk made a dozen quick gestures, at least half of which would have been grounds for battle if performed by anyone other than a wizard.

A mist formed about the dragon's-blood stain; the rest of the sword melted into the mist. In the pentacle a tiny dragon suddenly appeared, hissing and ill-tempered, with a bandage around its left foreclaw.

"You ain't got nuthin' on me!" snarled the creature.

"Speak!" Marduk said. The dragon belched brimstone and turned its back. Marduk began to chant in a thin dry voice of unspeakable things. The dragon hunched its shoulders and wrapped its head in its wings.

"Speak!" Marduk said again.

The dragon made a gesture in Marduk's direction Halfdan found insulting, but Marduk only raised his chant to a higher level. The air in the room turned smoky blue.

In a few moments the dragon, smoking and bubbling like a leaky alembic, cried for mercy. "Lighten up, boss," pleaded the dragon. "I'll talk. I was only following orders. He woulda skinned me alive if I hadn'ta."

"No sniveling! Who would?"

"It was Zark, boss, Zark of the Golden Tower, he's behind all this. 'Go fetch me the virgin daughter of a ruling nobleman,' he says, and he threatens to stick me in the basement and heat his tower with me for the next three winters if I don't. So I took off and I hang around this tavern and I hear stories about this Baron with a kid he won't let a man near, and I wait for him and grab the kid."

"Is the lady alive still?" asked Marduk.

"Well, I think so," whined the dragon. "I didn't stay around once he took her off my hands."

"If he's hurt her — " began Halfdan indignantly.

"Silence!" ordered Marduk. "Why didn't you kill the lady's father when he cut you with his sword?," he asked the dragon.

The dragon hissed like a new horseshoe plunged into cold water. "Zark warned me not to, so I didn't, even though he like to took off my hand." The dragon held up the bandaged appendage.

Marduk looked at Wulfstan. "I don't like this," he said. "Zark is extremely powerful."

Wulfstan agreed, "We'll have to tread most carefully."

"Well, perhaps we can inquire further." Marduk made the magical gestures again, in reverse order. There was a tiny shriek from the pentacle as the small dragon melted away, leaving the sword to wobble for a moment, then fall. The stain on it had vanished, and the blade gleamed like new. *That's something, at least*, thought Halfdan.

Halfdan and the two wizards went back into the comfortable living room and Marduk served up more of the hot beverage, which he explained was a brew of roasted mountain berries from a distant land.

"Zark of the Golden Tower is a specialist in war," said Marduk. "I fear for your daughter's safety. His kind of spells tend to use up the ingredients very thoroughly." He thought. "The virgin daughter of a ruling nobleman. That sounds like a conjuring spell."

The baron bowed his head. "Will she die?"

Marduk said simply, "Perhaps it would be best to hope so. War-mongers play with devils and demons. Would you want your daughter to be given as a plaything to one of those?"

Halfdan's heart grew cold. "No, I suppose not." She was young and very pretty, and not a bad sort of creature, for a girl. She sang merrily and rode well, and had taken over many of the more wearisome tasks of running the barony. He'd miss her. "Can't we go take her? Zark's stronghold is only a few leagues from here."

Wulfstan said instantly — he didn't like switching owners too frequently — "No, no; I can't recommend going up against Zark. He's far too good at what he does."

"I agree," said Marduk. "I think we'd better call in a specialist in demons for consultation."

After a quick scan by way of a candle flame, they found Beo of Lutetia was visiting Aelfric, the telekinesis specialist; so they called on Marduk's crystal and were invited over.

Beo was a splendid sight, if a trifle excessive in dress and manner. He was a short, plump eunuch in a flowing gown of red and gold, green and lavender, brown and blue, depending on which side he presented. He was wearing a turban with a peacock feather held front and center in a golden clasp. Halfdan disliked him on sight. He didn't care for eunuchs, was beginning not to care for specialists. This one looked even more expensive than Marduk.

Marduk introduced Beo as one of the world's greatest practitioners in a demanding field. Beo giggled archly, and eyed Halfdan's purse.

"'Demanding' is the word for it," Halfdan murmured to Wulfstan with a groan. "The gods grant this oily clothes-horse knows his business as well as Marduk says."

With Beo was a tall, wild-eyed Arab in a tattered robe. "A colleague of mine," the eunuch said. "Abdul Alhazred, on a pilgrimage gathering material for a book he's writing. He's also a demonologist."

The wizards huddled, muttered, and conjured. Mists with glowing eyes of many colors appeared and dissipated. Under Aelfric's spells the transparent forms of other wizards appeared and gestured together with Marduk, Beo, and Abdul; while Wulfstan watched with sheer enchantment, and Halfdan, in a daze, produced gold coins as demanded.

The room darkened and took on a sulfurous odor. More pentacles were drawn, and demons came and went as great thundering invocations were made. Abdul Alhazred performed a conjuration that vaporized full seven pieces of gold.

At long last windows were opened. Fresh air and late afternoon sunshine stole into the great hall. The five wizards, and Halfdan, were alone. The wizards nodded together then came over to the Baron.

Marduk spoke first. "Zark intends to make a Midsummer Eve sacrifice of your daughter to the Demon Lord Zabibbo, thus gaining command over all the demons in Zabibbo's legions. It is a long, complex, difficult, demanding conjuration, and none of us would dare attempt it, much less try to stop it. We are a little surprised that even Zark should attempt it. If the sacrifice isn't exactly as advertised, Zabibbo will tear Zark to shreds."

"The dragon was under orders not to damage you," Wulfstan put in, "because the orphan of a nobleman doesn't count. Zabibbo is an extremely particular demon."

"But this is Midsummer's Eve!" groaned Baron Halfdan, covering his face with his hands. "Can't we do something?"

"Well . . ." said Marduk, "you could kill yourself."

"Seeing as how we can't do anything about the virgin end of it," smirked Beo.

Halfdan frowned. "I can't really see how killing myself would be much of a solution," he said.

"Perhaps it's not quite as bad as that," said Wulfstan, producing parchment, quill and ink from thin air. "I'm only a general practitioner, but I think I have an idea." He explained what must be done.

"That shave-tail?" shouted Halfdan. "Never!"

But after a few minutes thought about the shabby but comfortable castle that would nevermore ring with a merry voice, and a brown mare disconsolate in the stables, he sighed and took the quill in hand. Wulfstan dictated the formula. Fortunately, the writing was brief, for Halfdan was more warrior than scholar. He scrawled his signature on the badly blotted page just as the sun was dipping below the horizon.

The instant he pressed his signet-ring into the pool of wax, making the document legal, the air was rent with a distant hideous scream that grew louder until the room filled with an agonized orange color. The wizards paled and made furtive gestures. A darkness followed, one that devoured the orange light. A probing angry chill crawled along Halfdan's bones. But the presence slowly left, and candles pipped into flame in the wall sconces.

A familiar whap-whap-whap was heard outside the window, in the courtyard. Halfdan ran to look out.

"Daddy!" shrieked a glad voice. Whap-whap-whap, went the hurried dragon's wings back over the wall.

"Halla!" he shouted. "Are you well?"

"A little smoky! Daddy, I've had the most interesting time! Wait till you hear!"

Halfdan smiled. Brave child. Good thing the marriage contract was already signed. He'd have to move in with his son-in-law, because he'd resigned his baronetcy to his half brother William in order that Halla no longer be the daughter of a ruler. William wouldn't want him underfoot, with his own ideas of how the barony should be run.

He wondered if Aethelwold would allow him to bring Wulfstan along. It had been the wizard's idea for Halfdan to resign, and a mind capable of such subtleties might prove useful in the years to come. For Halfdan did NOT intend to sit idle before Aethelwold's fire .

THE OLD SHELL GAME

Potiphar Pugh and the fossil man bent over the table: the one in the back, where the dirty work was done.

"Pete," the fossil man said, "you're used to plaster. Open up the package, some of it spills on the table. Measure it out, more spills. Stir it up and pour it, and you have a bowl to clean."

"Now here," he continued, "we have a whole 'nother kettle of fish." He held up a small plastic cup, like a pudding cup, and peeled the foil cover back. It was half-full of a tan powder.

"Each cup is sealed, so you don't have to worry about it going bad. Open it, pour water in up to this line, and give it a few stirs with a Popsicle stick. I include the stick in the package. You don't need a separate catalyst."

Potiphar watched with interest as the fossil man poured the creamy substance into a small rubber mold. "How fast does it set up?" he asked.

"You can handle it in four minutes," the fossil man replied, nonchalantly dumping the rest of the cupful onto the table. It looked quite at home among the earlier marks of plaster and paint, soldering irons and cutting knives. Potiphar winced, but only a little; this table was for messes, after all.

"You see, it's mostly powdered stone, mixed in with polymers that are activated by water. Solid as a rock after about ten minutes; and I defy you to tell it from the real thing. Comes in limestone and shale, and you can tint it with acrylic paints for a better color match. I'm working on sandstone, but so far it's not cooperating."

He glanced at his watch, and picked up the rubber mold. He worked it briefly, and a small trilobite popped out. "There, Pete, what did I tell you? There's not one rockhound in ten could tell it from a real fossil without turning it over to see the mold opening.

"And here's a bonus: most synthetic rock, you need something God-awful like toluene for cleanup. Mineral spirits wipe my formulation up like a charm." He poured paint thinner on a cloth, and attacked the smear of "rock" on the table. And while the charm obviously involved quite a bit of elbow grease, in two minutes the rock was gone, while the earlier plaster stains remained.

Potiphar was turning the freshly-minted trilobite over and over, examining it closely. "Fred, that is amazing," he said. "The kids that come through the Touch and Feel room could use those little cups with no trouble. And that's one of the best rubber molds I've seen. What all do you have?"

"Oh, another trilobite; a brachiopod, a small ammonite, a crinoid, several different fish skeletons – the crowd pleasers."

Potiphar stood. "You've sold me," he said. "I'll take two sets of the molds, and a gross each of the limestone and the shale mixing cups. Do you have larger quantities of the rock mix? I'm working on an exhibit."

"Sure do," the fossil man replied as they went to the door. "There's a fifty pound sack of the limestone mix in the back of the jeep. It's been opened and I've used some – I'll let you have it half-price."

The jeep in front of the museum was battered with hard use. Carefully locked in a tool-rack were pickaxes, shovels, mattocks. Water and gasoline cans were bolted in carriers. A sign painted on the door proclaimed "Fred Wilson Fossil Expedition". Wilson himself wore khaki and engineer boots, topped by a bushranger hat almost as battered as the jeep. A cynical observer might, perhaps, snort at such theatricality.

They were theatrical. Fred Wilson was the fossil man, and don't you forget it. And yet − Wilson's face was an outdoorsman's face. There was reality behind the facade. Potiphar was a naturalist, well able to recognize another citizen of the wilderness.

Wilson opened a weathertight storage chest, and handed Potiphar two large cases of rock-powder cups; then added a small box of rubber molds. As he hoisted the 50-pound sack onto his shoulder, a yellow bus turned into the drive, resounding of children.

"Fred, could you take that sack back to the workroom, and then have Sally issue you a check for this stuff? I want to try these molds out, and here are just the customers. Digger Dan's out today, so I'm holding down the Touch and Feel Room." And Potiphar hurried back into the museum.

An hour later the room was still surprisingly clean, with only a scatter of mixing cups. The kids were reassembling into travelling order. In the back a fifth-grade shyster was bargaining his way to a complete set of the replica fossils they'd just made; but most of the children had put them away at their teacher's request. Chattering and squealing, they headed out for the bus.

At the door, Mrs. Anderson spotted the shyster's bulging pockets, saw a trilobite peeking out. (She'd been a junior-high library monitor for fifteen years when Potiphar hired her away from the school system. Nothing got by her.)

She swelled to twice life-size, and swept out to intercept the malefactor. "It's okay, Mrs. Anderson," Potiphar called out. "He made them himself. One of them, anyhow... Could you show them to Mrs. Anderson, Samuel?"

Samuel dug in his pockets, and laid his treasures in a neat line on Mrs. Anderson's desk. She clucked and exclaimed over them; "My word, you had me fooled! I thought for sure you were walking off with some of the real fossils we keep in the back!" Samuel grinned and blushed at the praise, and in relief at the close escape; then was snagged and hustled off by the teacher. The bus doors accordioned shut, and it rolled onto the highway with children waving out of the windows at Potiphar and Mrs. Anderson as they stood in the drive.

"Went real well," Potiphar said. "The Fossil Man sold me some new molds, and I was trying them out. I think it'll be a good activity to have, kids making their own fossils. We'll see how Digger Dan likes the idea — he's the one that'll have to live with it."

Potiphar turned, and the Fossil Man was behind him. "Borrowed the office phone while I was in there," Wilson said. "I checked with the freight company, and I've got some nice Green River Formation fossils arriving late Friday. I have to be in Chicago Monday, but if we could get together Saturday I could let you have a look.

"Also, I've got a chunk of mammoth tusk knocking around; not worth exhibiting, but the kids would love it. Buy something, save me from having to haul it to Chicago, and I could throw in the tusk."

"I'll be by at ten, Saturday," he said as he got into his jeep and roared off, not giving Potiphar a chance to say no.

"That's Fred Wilson all over," said Mrs. Anderson sympathetically. "I hope you haven't got much planned for Saturday."

The museum was quiet and empty. Late-afternoon sun slanted in as Potiphar made his accustomed rounds: checking windows, turning off lights, making sure doors were locked. He loved this routine, silently moving among his treasures. A patch of white against the far wall: a snow goose mounted on a hummock, painted prairie marsh fading into the distance behind it. And ahead was the flickering blue underwater light of the largemouth bass diorama. (How long had it taken to get that light just right?)

He went through the archway into the next room, and his heart skipped a beat at the hulking shadow poised to lunge at him. "That damn wild boar!" he thought. No matter how many times he saw it, it startled him. The taxidermist had done a wonderful and fearsome job.

Something was wrong. In the room beyond, the door to the "Fossil Treasures" display case was slightly ajar. Potiphar covered the distance in three strides.

The golden pyrite sand dollars were still there; the polished slab of turitella-stone and the huge agate disk of petrified wood remained. But the centerpiece of the display − the ammonite shell, almost a foot across and petrified into shining opal, polished into iridescent beauty, was gone! His favorite exhibit!

What had happened to the alarm? He bent for a closer look. A tiny bar magnet lay upon the magnetic switch, keeping it from noting the door's opening. He ran to the front door, locked the deadbolt − now anyone in the museum would stay there. There was no way out of the building without a key.

He went to the alarm console, reset the motion detectors, and waited anxiously. If anybody was in the museum, he wasn't moving. Potiphar set out to check the museum for − visitors.

And found none.

He checked every room. He checked the secret places all museums have, and the public places, and he locked the doors behind him as he went. There was nobody in the men's room, and there was nobody in the women's. (He didn't even hesitate.)

The alarm system had recorded his progress faithfully; it still worked. There was one last place to check.

Whenever something disappears in a museum frequented by children, the staff searches the bushes by the exit. Sometimes children will get carried away playing cops-and-robbers, but the game plan doesn't go beyond that. Once they've stolen something, been the badman, they dispose of the evidence at the first possible opportunity. That's usually the bushes just outside.

Potiphar searched, and found the stuffed robin from the "City Soil" exhibit. It had been missing for weeks, and was in dreadful shape. There were cigarette butts and gum wrappers. There was no fossil.

He searched the bushes around the side of the house, and the back, and the far side. Then he began to search the perimeter of the grounds. Pheasant's nest back in the bushes; rabbit trail; a family of skunks had been by, leaving a pattering of tiny footprints in a patch of mud from last night's rain. No traces on the only passable trail down the bluff at the rear; and suddenly he fetched up at the side of the highway.

He grabbed himself by the cerebral scruff of his neck, and shook. "Stop stewing around, and call the cops," he told himself. And he did.

Soon two police cars pulled up and uniformed men got out, one from each car. Potiphar explained the problem, and the museum's security arrangements. One began a close inspection of the yard, while the other went indoors with Potiphar to examine the alarms and the display case. They quickly decided the job needed a detective, equipped with fingerprint kit, camera, and specialized training.

Captain Neill wore plainclothes and carried a toolkit of medium size. He huddled briefly with the patrolmen, then spoke with Potiphar for some while, concentrating on the security precautions normally used by the museum. Finally he asked the obvious question: "Just why would anybody want to steal a fossil, Mr. Pugh?"

"Most fossils, only a collector would want. But this one was different." Potiphar pointed to the case next to "Fossil Treasures", and a spiraling shell perhaps the size of a grapefruit.

"The pearly nautilus," he said. "Many people consider it to be the most beautiful shell on Earth. The ammonites looked a lot like it. But this ammonite lived about 200 million years ago.

"A lot can happen to a fossil in that time. Sometimes the original material is replaced by minerals: that's how you get petrified wood. The original shell of the ammonite dissolved away, and was replaced by opal. That isn't uncommon — but in this case, it was gem-quality opal."

"We had it polished, and we built a room's worth of exhibits around it. We have it insured for fifty thousand dollars; God only knows how much it could be sold for. And I can easily think of several people who would buy it, no questions asked."

"Oh," said Neill. He held up his hands, fingertips touching, to make a ball in the air. "An opal jewel, this big?"

"Bigger."

"Now that I know why they stole it, I got just one question. How did they sneak it out the door?"

"That's driving me up the wall," agreed Potiphar. "Nobody gets anything past Mrs. Anderson. The alarm system shows the emergency doors haven't been opened all day — and unlike this display, the doors are steel-covered. That would block any outside magnets from affecting the magnetic switches. Last year we painted all the ground-floor windows shut when we finally got the air conditioning."

Neill chuckled. "More secure than locking them."

He frowned. "You said Mrs. Anderson was at her desk by the door all day; but nobody is at their desk *all* day. Our thief may simply have waited until she was away for a minute, and gotten it out then.

"In any case, I can't do much with a floor that has been walked on all day by hundreds of people. Let's test the alarm system sensors, and then I'll go over the inside of the display case for fingerprints."

The sensors all worked, and the only prints inside the case belonged to Potiphar. Neill shrugged, and repacked his case. "We'll put out a bulletin — it'll be hard to sell something that spectacular, and if the thief's not a professional we could get him that way. Would you have a picture of the missing fossil?"

Potiphar got several postcards from the souvenir rack. "Faith, that's pretty!" said Neill; and Potiphar murmured agreement.

Neill left, promising to keep the Museum informed of developments. Potiphar was alone in the darkened halls.

He set the alarms and let himself out, then crossed the courtyard to the carriage house where he lived. The entire property had once been his ancestral home; but he was the last of his line. And while he had an independent income, the mere well-to-do can no longer afford Stately Homes.

As a naturalist, he had known the Wilderness Foundation was looking for a home for the museum they hoped to build. He had sold the house to them, with a five-year contract for himself as curator thrown in, and had proceeded to build a fine small museum. The mansion was − if anything − more completely his now than it had been when he was living there. And it had been violated.

Potiphar ate a tasteless meal from an aluminum tray, not noticing it. His mind scurried about, retracing his steps as he searched the museum and grounds; and he found no more in memory than he had in person.

He turned on the television for distraction. That proved to be a terrible idea: the evening movie was a museum-heist story. Potiphar turned it off and went to bed, slipping into an uneasy slumber filled with dreams of cat-burglars suspended like spiders from ropes to the skylights his museum had somehow acquired.

The next day, Potiphar prowled the halls of the museum, startling the occasional visitor as he popped out of strange and unsuspected doors. The evening before, he'd been looking for a thief; today, he was looking for clues.

Mrs. Anderson sat at her desk by the door, watching even more carefully than usual. Sally, in the office, went through draft after draft of a report to the Foundation board.

The only person having a normal day was Digger Dan in the Touch and Feel Room. It was Friday, and that meant kids. Normally they felt the beaver pelt, held box turtles from the aquarium, wore the pheasant-skin as a hat, and pawed through a small collection of fossils and shells. Today, Dan had them making fossils in his little workshop. They loved it.

During a break in the action, Dan caught Potiphar as he emerged from a walkway hidden between the beaver diorama and the birds' eggs. "Pete, the kids love the stuff you got for the Room yesterday, especially those fossil molds. We've gone through half a case of that fake rock already!"

"Good," said Potiphar, pleased. "but we can't afford to let them make fossils for free after today. Talk with the teachers, Dan, and see if you can't work this into a course the schools would be willing to pay for."

A chatter of high voices rose up as the front door opened, and Dan made a dash for his sanctum. Potiphar shook his head, grateful *somebody* could behave normally. Today he could only think of his missing shell. Tomorrow, maybe.... Yeah, that would be Fred Wilson with some fresh fossils. The Show Must Go On.

Potiphar crossed the room and unlocked a hinged section of wall. He stepped through the opening, flashlight in hand, and pulled the wall closed behind him.

He was standing in a narrow passage with rough-framed irregular walls on either side: the backs of exhibits. From the right, he heard young voices exclaiming over the wild boar that had startled him so, just before this began. His flashlight showed footprints in the dust before him, leading into the dark; a clue! He followed them, to where they formed a scuffed spot behind a recessed light fixture. He cursed softly; he'd made those prints himself, a month ago, when he changed the bulbs. Another dead end.

Potiphar sat, feet on his desk, lost in thought. He'd gone over the museum, searched every hidden nook and cranny, and there were no clues to be found. The opal ammonite had vanished without a trace.

How could anybody have gotten it past Mrs. Anderson? He tried to imagine a seventh-grader, staggering under the burden of a 35-pound fossil, evading her x-ray stare. For a minute he pictured birdlike Mrs. Anderson carrying it out; and that was even more improbable. Formidable though she was, she was seventy; and she operated on force of personality, not physical strength.

Kids were out, Mrs. Anderson was out. Who else was there? Dan? The Fossil Man? A teacher? He frowned. And how? It might be possible to just walk out the door with it — but that would take more luck, timing, and gall than most people could muster.

Sally knocked, and came in with a sheaf of papers. "I've tried writing a letter to the Board," she said. "How's this?

"On Thursday, May 24, the Wildlife Museum was faced with the most serious crisis in its existence to date, when its magnificent and priceless opal shell was deftly stolen under the very nose of...."

Potiphar raised his open hand with a wry laugh. "Sally, I've been acting like this is our most serious crisis, so I can't blame you for saying so, but it's not. What about the time the pipes burst in the collections storage room? Or that lawsuit over the Harris accession?"

Sally blushed. She wanted to be a writer — Potiphar had read a number of her efforts — and she had a weakness for hyperbole.

"Try to mellow it out a bit, hey? We don't want to stampede the board, and above all we want to watch what ideas we put in their head. Just be very careful not to say anything beyond what's there to be said...."

Potiphar's feet crashed to the floor, and he sat bolt upright. "Beyond what's there!" he cried, and was out of his office like a shot.

"Dan!" he shouted, bursting into the Touch and Feel Room, setting off shrieks among startled fourth graders. "You said the kids liked the things I'd gotten your room, *especially* the fossil molds. But the molds are the *only* thing I got!"

"Then where did that fat limestone ammonite come from, over on the fossil table?" Dan said, pointing. "I knew you saw Fred Wilson yesterday, so I figured you got it from him."

Potiphar whirled, stared, then with a glad "Aha!" snatched up the ammonite, and headed for his workshop at a run. Fifteen minutes and a pint of mineral spirits later, the thin layer of imitation limestone was gone and the opal ammonite lay revealed to view.

Potiphar stamped into his office, temporarily more a force of nature than its curator. "Hold the letter, Sally; things have changed!" he called out as he dialed Capt. Neill's number.

"The way I see it, Fred Wilson knew how much that fossil was worth," he told the detective an hour later, as a puzzled Neill looked at the glowing shell. "There he was, alone in the museum with the ammonite and an open sack of imitation limestone. He knew I would be busy with the kids for at least twenty minutes, so he popped the case open, took the shell back to my shop, and gave it a quick coat of stone to make it look like an ordinary fossil.

"Then when I was out seeing the kids off, he nipped into the Touch and Feel Room and put it on the fossil table. He figured nobody would notice it there."

"If he had magnets with him, he might have been planning this for some time," Captain Neill noted.

"Yes," said Potiphar, "and was just waiting for his chance. So let's go pick him up."

"Well, we've got a problem with that. You see, he didn't steal your ammonite. There it is, on your desk. And I don't think we could prove attempted theft."

Potiphar fumed. "But he's a crook! He's coming back tomorrow – Saturday, when Mrs. Anderson isn't at the door – to steal it. What do you want me to do, let him take it? What if he gets away?" He ran a loving finger over his prize. "No. This is too precious to risk."

Neill sighed. "Yeah, I understand. Maybe we'll catch him next time."

A crafty smile slowly spread across Potiphar's face. "Still, it would be a shame to disappoint him," he said.

Potiphar watched from his office window as Fred Wilson loaded crates into the jeep. The museum now owned several new Cretaceous fishes (if the word "new" can be applied to something from the Age of Dinosaurs) and there was an interesting if battered piece of mammoth tusk in the Touch and Feel Room.

And after Fred Wilson had taken away the crate he'd brought the tusk in, a large limestone ammonite fossil was gone.

The jeep pulled out onto highway 13, headed west. "He's off the museum property," Potiphar thought, and spoke into the transceiver Captain Neill had given him.

Two police cars shot from side streets, neatly boxing the jeep between them. Potiphar ran out the door, and reached Wilson just in time to hear Neill finish reading him his rights.

Wilson was cool, no denying it. When they opened up the crate, he shrugged. "Of course I've got fossils in the jeep! I'm the Fossil Man. Open up the other crates, and you'll find more."

"You stole my ammonite!" Potiphar growled between clenched teeth. He snatched it from the case, and thrust it in Wilson's face.

"Nonsense!" Wilson replied reasonably. "Your ammonite is opalized. Mine is perfectly ordinary limestone."

Potiphar snarled as if enraged, and moved to grab Wilson. Neill blocked him; Potiphar lost his footing. His arms waved, seeking balance, and the fossil flew into the air.

"Jesus Christ!" Wilson screamed, diving to catch it. "Don't you know how delicate opal is?" The fossil hit the road, and a small chunk broke off.

Potiphar and Captain Neill shook hands, while Wilson looked unbelievingly at the loose, drab piece of stone.

"I believe that counts as a confession. And he said it spontaneously, so it should be admissible," Neill said.

"You were expecting opal all over the road, weren't you?" Potiphar said icily. "Let's try it again, shall we?"

He hurled the ammonite to the pavement with all his strength. It burst into a thousand pieces. A plastic Ziploc bag was partially embedded in one of the larger chunks.

Potiphar picked up the chunk with the bag, and flipped the plastic with his finger directly in front of Wilson's nose. It contained a postcard of the opal ammonite, Potiphar's business card, and several large bills.

"See that?" he asked. "Two hundred fifty dollars makes it a felony. You may not have stolen the opal, but by God, you're not getting out of this one on a technicality!"

Potiphar looked the Fossil Man in the eye. "You aren't the only one who knows how to make rubber molds," he said. "You're looking at the rest of your sack of limestone powder, down there around your feet.

"Do business with me for years, then stab me in the back? I wish they still had the old rockpile, so the other jailbirds could see a real professional rockhound at work!"

Potiphar watched as the police car bore Fred Wilson into the distance. "Damn," he said softly to himself. "The kids really loved making those fossils.

"I hope I can find another supplier for that special rock, now that the Fossil Man is out of business."

THOROLF AND THE PEACOCK

When Thorolf Pike was outlawed from Surtsheim District because of some killings, he decided he would go live among the English. A number of his supporters were outlawed along with him. They loaded all their valuables onto Thorolf's knorr and sailed away in a great hurry, before their enemies could combine and come at them.

There were fourteen of them, all bachelors like the Jomsvikings, and the ship could have been very crowded. However, most had suspected the judgment of the Althing would go against them, and they'd sold many of their possessions. They wore lots of silver, and had more in their chests; otherwise, they travelled light.

They made port at Northlanding, a border town where the people were a mix of English and Welsh. Thorolf had traded there before, and knew quite a few of the merchants. He had a handsome assortment of furs on board, and sold them for a good profit.

They pooled their riches, with Thorolf providing the lion's share, and bought a strong warehouse with a greathall upstairs, and outbuildings in a fenced-in yard. It was in the heart of the merchant district, near the road down the bluffs to the docks. Then they all went to the cathedral and got themselves primsigned so good Christians could trade more comfortably with them.

The bishop apparently expected more from this polite fiction than most churchmen, and was grievously offended when Thorolf and the others failed to attend services. This disfavor in high places made some of the locals uncomfortable. Others set more store by the quality of Thorolf's wares.

Thorolf was a good businessman and a formidable bargainer; and one of his men, Otkel, was as sly as the King of the Foxes. By making lots of advantageous deals — aided by the threat implicit in his exile for killings — Thorolf was soon on his way to becoming one of the richest merchants in the town.

Though he took on some English manners, Thorolf kept many Norse ways: he was very hospitable, and gave rich presents to his friends and supporters. Many merchants guested in Thorolf's hall; ate and drank freely and emerged wearing gifts of silver. They often had been skinned in trade — but that was business, which Thorolf kept strictly apart from hospitality.

One morning Thorolf and his men were riding along the bluffs when they saw a ship putting in to the docks below. It was brightly painted, and the sails were gaily dyed; banners flew from the masthead.

"That's a handsome ship," Thorolf said. "And it looks like it would carry cargo well. I wonder who owns it."

"The banners belong to Jonathan Draper," said Leif, who'd learned something of heraldry. "He makes clothing for wealthy nobles and merchants. He travels about, gathering up fabrics and furs and fashions, and gossip. He's a favorite of the court and extremely rich, and folk say he thinks himself one of the most important people beneath Heaven."

"Many people feel that way about themselves," Thorolf said. "With his connections at court, it'd help our standing here no end if he stayed with us, and we might do business with him. There's fine ermine in our warehouse, and beaver and martin. Leif, go down there and offer him our hospitality."

By the time Leif made his way down the zigzag bluff road, the crew had begun to unload the ship. They were putting up an enormous pavilion tent in bright stripes of blue and yellow, in a nearby field reserved for such uses. Jonathan Draper stood watching, surrounded by six armed men.

Jonathan himself was slight of build, with a dissipated face and a tailor's stoop. He wore a riding houppelande of midnight blue strewn with embroidered flowers in gold. His shoes had points a foot long, held up by fine golden chains rising to garters of Morocco leather at his knees. The bodyguards were clothed in black silk and leather; they wore polished helmets, and shirts of silvered mail. Leif was dressed prosperously, but suddenly felt shabby by comparison.

He dismounted, and inclined his head courteously. "Have I the honor of addressing Jonathan Draper?" he asked.

The magnificent apparition looked at Leif, and sniffed. "You do have that honor," he agreed.

"Well then," Leif continued, "Thorolf Pike invites you to be a guest in his greathall, you and your men. Thorolf is one of the richest merchants in Northlanding, and his halls are much more comfortable than a tent this close to the water. We've fine furs in the warehouse beneath, which a man of your discrimination will surely want to examine at leisure."

"I know of Thorolf, and his furs," Jonathan said. "I'll be glad to see the furs in the marketplace. But why in the world should I want to share a large and smoky room with a killer barbarian who's been cast out even by the other barbarians? My fine pavilion will be more comfortable." He turned to shout instructions at his overseer, supervising the erection of the tent. It really was a beautiful tent.

Leif's face turned red as his beard. He reached for his sword, but the six guards closed ranks about Jonathan. Leif hooked his thumb in his belt as if that were what he intended to do all along. The guards snickered, hands on their sword-hilts, as Leif remounted and rode away.

As he left, he saw Brother Maynard, the Bishop's chief clerk, heading towards the camp-grounds.

Leif explained all this to Thorolf, who swore by Odin and Thor that the clothier would regret his words. "But maybe the best god of all for this revenge is Loki," he said. "Otkel, find that man's weak spot."

Otkel smiled crookedly, and left.

He returned late that evening. Most of the men had made up their beds and were getting ready for sleep when they heard a crash downstairs, and the door slammed. Slow uneven steps came up the stairs, and Otkel staggered into the room. He was drunk as a lord, and grinning. He collapsed, one joint folding at a time, onto a heap of furs.

"Got'm!" he said, as Thorolf came out of his room and hurried over. "Got one of his cooks drunk, 'n how he did talk!"

"He's almost out of absinthe. He gets *awful* mean when he runs out. An' we c'ntrol th'only merchant in town what sells the stuff!" Otkel lay back.

"Absinthe – " Thorolf said to himself. "Drink enough of that, and it'll rot your mind. No wonder he's so unpleasant."

Otkel lifted his head. "Oh, som'thn else. Bishop's man came with invite, and Jon'thn sent *him* packing too!" His head fell back on the furs, and he began to snore.

Thorolf laughed, it was so strange to find himself and the bishop cast adrift on the same seas.

Two men dressed in black, with polished armor, came trotting down the road and stopped to speak with an unkempt peasant lounging nearby.

"Where can we find the best doctor in Northlanding?" one of them asked. "Our master has been taken suddenly ill."

The peasant scrambled to his feet. "If you be in a hurry, this be the shortest way." He set off down a barely-visible side trail. The two guards followed.

As they were going through a patch of thick bushes, half-a-dozen ruffians leaped on the guards. A few swift blows, and they were unconscious; the peasants began to strip them. A length of rope, some sailors' knots, and the naked men were trussed up like geese and rolled into the bushes.

Soon a litter, carried by four men in livery, arrived at the pavilion. A mounted man, in a more elaborate version of the livery, called out. "Hello! Is this the camp of Jonathan Draper?"

A servant came out. "It is, but he's dreadfully ill, sir."

"Why yes, that's why my master, the physician Jeremiah, sent me. Tell me, did he start sweating first? Was this followed by vomiting, and stomach cramps?"

"Why, yes, m'lord. He'd just had lunch, and was complaining about the quality of the local absinthe, when it started just like you say."

"Then there's no time to waste. He's got the green-sickness, and needs sweating and fumigation. My master is having the steam bath prepared at this very moment. Bring your master out − we brought a litter for him."

Two servants half-carried the clothier out of the pavilion. His hair was damp and plastered to his head; his skin was pale, and he moaned. He'd soiled his houppelande. The servants lifted him onto the litter, and he flopped back against the cushions.

The bearers adjusted the weight on their shoulders, and started up the road at a trot. The guards came along, two on either side of the litter, and the rider followed.

As they were going among some isolated bushes, one of the bearers stumbled. The litter lurched and swayed, and the clothier moaned and retched as he held on for dear life. The guards swiftly reached for the litter to save their master from a fall; and as they were occupied, a band of peasants leaped on them and overpowered them before they could draw their weapons.

Truncheons flew, and the guards and the merchant fell unconscious. They were stripped and tied up; their goods and clothing were loaded onto the litter. One of the peasants tried to get on the litter with the goods, but the bearers tilted him out onto the ground. The bunch of them laughed heartily, and carried the litter and its load off.

Thorolf Pike and six others were going down to the docks with a wagon full of cloth when they saw several men lying on the ground beside the trail, naked and all tied up. A couple were writhing about, furiously cursing as they tried to undo their bonds; two were unconscious. The fifth was sick, and moaning; he scarcely fought the ropes at all.

"What's this?" Thorolf said. "Untie them!" He himself went towards the sick man, knife in hand, and cut away his bonds. "What's happened?" he asked.

One of the guards spluttered out a story about peasants and robbers, and their master being ill. Thorolf stood, lifting the sick man like a feather. They quickly rearranged the cloth in the wagon, making it into an impromptu bed. They lifted the men in, and covered them over.

"Let's get these men back to the greathall. Leif, ride ahead and fetch a doctor for them."

One of the guards raised his head. "There are two more of us," he said. "I don't know where. The robbers may have gotten them, too."

Thorolf detailed two of his men to search for the other guards. They drove the wagon ahead until they reached a wide spot in the road, and turned it around; then they headed for their hall as rapidly as they could.

Servants gathered about, and carried the men inside. They quickly lay out bolsters in the greathall, and covered the invalids with warm furs to rest. Thorolf took the merchant into his own room, and put him down on his own bed of precious white bear-furs from the land of the Finns. He set a silver basin by the man's head, just in case, and brought him soothing herbal wines until the doctor could arrive.

The doctor gave the clothier a tincture of poppy to make him sleep, then spread unguents on the bruises and abrasions of the guards. "They should be fine, with a good night's rest," he said. Then Thorolf's men brought in the remaining two guards, and the doctor ministered to them also before he left. Soon, all were resting comfortably.

Thorolf slept that night in the greathall with his men and with the merchant's guards. He was up early, making sure the cook prepared a good meal for his guests; and he took broth and bread into the merchant with his own hands.

After Jonathan had eaten, Thorolf said, "Now, we found you and your men naked, and I can't have that. I want you to take your pick of my finest clothing." He went to his chest and held up his best clothes for the merchant's inspection. None of them were the silk Jonathan loved, but they were woven from soft wool of excellent quality. There were decorative bands at the neck and hem and sleeves, brightly-colored animals with long legs and necks intertwined in intricate knotwork.

Jonathan was a master of his craft. He could recognize these as fine work, even in a style he didn't favor. He picked a cream tunic with red animals outlined in couched gold thread, and bright yellow breeches. Thorolf gave him a red belt and boots to go with it, and a pouch with a dagger in a worked-in scabbard. When he was dressed, Jonathan suddenly realized he felt fine, without a trace of illness.

"You've had a hard time of it," Thorolf said to him. "Tomorrow is soon enough for you to get back to your work. You should rest in our solar. It's on the south end of the greathall."

They went together into the hall, and Jonathan was surprised to see his men up and dressed. They were all wearing white linen, with embroidered stags in black. They had black breeches and boots, and a black belt. The captain of his guard was going through an intricate sword-drill, while everybody watched from a safe distance. The blade flickered and gleamed in the morning light coming through a window.

"My lord!" he called out, when he recognized Jonathan in the strange clothing. "Look how they've outfitted us! They've given me a very good sword, and the men too!" His sword danced into a salute, and he bowed to Jonathan and Thorolf, who were standing together.

"Maybe these swords will serve you better than the ones I bought you," Jonathan said sourly. His memory of the previous day was coming back. "Get down to the pavilion, and see what's happening there."

Thorolf and Jonathan were in the solar, swapping tales of unusual merchant ventures, when the captain returned. "Terrible news, m'lord!" he said.

"I talked with the other encampment in the Merchants' Field, and they said we guards had been there about sundown to break camp. The bandits must have taken our clothing so they could impersonate us.

"Then the servants returned, saying the doctor's man had come back an hour or so after you left and told them you would be gone overnight. They said you and the doctor sent instructions to spend the night on the ship, because with green-sickness in camp it wouldn't be safe to sleep close to the ground. They were as surprised as we were to find everything gone.

"But at least all our merchandise is safe on board, and we're all alive." He bowed his head.

Before the merchant could erupt, Thorolf broke in. "That's terrible! You must stay here until we can work this out!" And Jonathan contented himself with sending one of Thorolf's men up to the castle to notify the bailiff of the theft.

Thorolf held a great feast that night, in Jonathan Draper's honor, and many merchants attended it. There was rich food in plenty; there were musicians, and jongleurs, and ale. Jonathan was very full and quite merry when he sank into his bed of furs that night.

The next day, after breakfast, Thorolf took Jonathan into the solar. "I'm afraid the word isn't very good," he said. "The bailiff hasn't found a trace of your property, or of the thieves. And I had a messenger at daybreak: a dozen of my relatives are going to be in town tomorrow, and expect to guest with me. They're my relatives — I can't refuse — but they're not the sort of Northmen a man of your refinement would find companionable."

"That *is* unsettling. You've been a wonderful host; I can't find words enough to thank you. But my pavilion is gone, and my ship is crowded. Where can I stay?"

"Well, I have a very good pavilion in my warehouse," Thorolf said. "As merchants, we should be able to come to some sort of accommodation."

They set to bargaining furiously. Thorolf had the upper hand, and the deal was very expensive for Jonathan. Eventually they reached an agreement, and Thorolf had the pavilion loaded onto a wagon, with several more wagons to bring back the merchandise in trade.

As Jonathan and his men were preparing to leave, Thorolf snapped his fingers and one of his men came forward with a wooden chest. Thorolf opened it, and said, "Your visit didn't start under the best auspices, but despite that I wouldn't want you to feel you've been slighted in any way. Among Northmen, it's the custom to gift honored guests as they are leaving." And he gave a silver ring to each of the guards, and personally put a silver torc around Jonathan's neck.

"Think of me, when you wear this," Thorolf said. The drover cracked his whip, and the little caravan got under way. After a while, the wagons returned with a rich load of merchandise.

They'd no sooner gotten everything into the warehouse, and the gates closed, when Jonathan Draper came storming up the street at the head of his men, their swords drawn. All the neighbors slammed their doors and barred their shutters.

Jonathan beat on the door to the warehouse with ineffectual fists. "Come out! Come out, you pirate!" he bawled. His men brandished their swords.

Thorolf opened the shutters on his second-floor window, and leaned out. "Eh, Jonathan? Back so soon?" He smiled benignly down.

"You sold me my own tent! You had it dyed green so I wouldn't recognize it, and you sold me my own tent! I knew it as soon as it was pitched!"

"I suppose I had new fittings made, so you wouldn't recognize the ironwork while you were examining the merchandise?" Thorolf waved his hand in dismissal. "I got that tent from a circus that came through here recently. The clown was in charge of the circus − isn't that strange? But there you have it. I got that tent from a clown. He certainly wasn't a master merchant like you, to judge by the bargain he drove."

And then Thorolf's men all took turns looking down at the peacock and his crew, in the Northern finery they'd been given, until the peacock's guards realized they were well outnumbered and quietly urged their master to leave. One of Thorolf's men mussed his hair and leaned out of the window to point, saying "if you be going to the docks, that be the shortest way" in a coarse voice.

Jonathan went straight to the Baron, of course, and swore out a great thundering complaint against Thorolf and his men for assault, and theft, and swindle. But they didn't have any really solid evidence. The only witness they could think of was the town dyer, and he and his workers had left on a sudden trip to buy cochineal.

When he was summoned to answer the complaint, Thorolf pointed out that he'd treated Jonathan and his guards very well, as anybody could see by looking at their clothes and as many prominent locals who'd been at the feast could testify. Furthermore, Jonathan's men had been milling about his residence waving swords and frightening the neighbors. Thorolf wasn't at all sure but what he should swear out a complaint over *that*.

Several good friends of the Baron had been hurt by court gossip started by Jonathan Draper, so he was already inclined against the man. When the bishop came and swore that he knew exactly the clown Thorolf meant, the Baron sent Jonathan packing.

On the voyage home, he eased his sorrows with absinthe, but immediately had a terrible attack of green-sickness. That was when he realized the wineseller might have had something to do with his troubles — but of course, by then it was far too late to re-open the complaint with a new witness.

Leif stood in the cool shadows of the cathedral, talking with Brother Maynard. "Thorolf would like it very much if you and the Bishop could come to a feast in our greathall soon."

"What?" said the Brother. "Eat in a smoky room with a killer barbarian?"

"It's really not a bad idea. Look what happened to the last person who refused the opportunity. We'll even let the bishop bless the occasion."

And the two men leaned on each others' shoulders and shook with laughter.

DANCES WITH WEREWOLVES

"My girlfriend says she's a werewolf, but I'm starting to wonder if she's not."

Len Scott smiled with the left half of his mouth. "This is a problem?" he said.

Paul Johnson shrugged. "I *like* werewolves." Len said nothing, so Paul continued. "I'm a rock-climber. I run marathons. I love the outdoors. It keeps me in good shape, makes me feel alive."

Len looked at the man sitting across his desk. He was perhaps thirty, strong and lean, tanned and vital. Handsome in a sun-beaten way. Definitely alive.

"There's nothing more alive than a werewolf under the full moon," Paul said. "That's only three nights a month, but it carries over. Most Weres live more intensely every day of the month. Why shouldn't I want to be around them?"

"There's the possibility of being eaten when the full moon rises."

"There's the possibility of falling from a cliff when I rock-climb, or getting eaten by a bear in the Boundary Waters. If I can have extreme sports, why not extreme friendship, or even extreme romance?"

Len spread his hands, and smiled with both sides of his mouth. "It's as good a reason as any. And I can see why you came to Scott and Scott. We specialize in the unusual.

"Before you hire us, we should discuss some details. Discretion, for instance. There's a lot of prejudice against Weres. Who can blame them for wanting to keep their double life a secret? I don't like to out a werewolf unless there's something pretty bad going on."

The left side of Len's mouth quirked upwards. "Otherwise, *I* could be eaten when the full moon rises."

"I can live with that," Paul said. "I just want to know if she's lying to me."

"Well, then. I'll assign my sister Lena to this. She's somewhat a creature of the night herself. Let's fill in the details …. "

First Night of the Moon

Lena cruised her Miata down Flying Cloud Drive in the late-afternoon light, her short, sandy hair ruffling in the breeze. To the left were the lowlands of the Minnesota River, a haven for wildlife; to the right, sparsely-inhabited bluffs. The sun was almost to the horizon before her; in the rear-view mirror, she could see the moon rising. The air carried the scent of greenery and water. Birds sang their evening songs.

She turned onto an access road slanting up the bluff and rolled into a spot beside a black Corvette with white striping. The lot was almost full, normal for a Were bar at sunset. If Weres came later they'd be in their skins, not driving - especially the first night of the full moon. Werewolves and gasoline didn't mix well.

The Outlook was a stone building that hugged the sloping ground, with one story on the uphill side splitting into two on the downhill. There was a patio by the lower story. She crossed to the entrance, rust tulip skirt and cream blouse flowing in the evening breeze. A necklace of gold-tone Celtic beads swayed with her motion.

She waited inside the door for her eyes to adjust from sunset to dimness. She knew other eyes were looking; she was five-nine, with the build of a gymnast. Let them look.

The room was filled, and the air surprisingly clear for a bar. There was a nervous buzz of conversation. People were drifting towards the changing rooms on the upper level. One of the women looked very much like Paul's photo of Erica Schmidt. Between the stairs up was a third, down into an empty dining-room with a window-wall looking out over the river gorge. Egrets were flying, sunset-red against dark waters in the evening light.

Lena went to the bar. She caught the attention of the bartender, an enormous shaggy man in a long brown tunic. *This must be the legendary Bjorn Njalsson*, she thought. "I'd like a hot beef bouillon, with a dash of Tabasco," she said.

As she sat sipping, the sound of feet and conversation diminished. Muffled growls came from the changing rooms. She squirmed uneasily on her barstool. Bjorn's arms and legs were shorter, his body longer, his head more massive. Her perceptions shifted; he'd become a bear.

He returned. "Haven't seen you here before," he said in a low, chuckling voice.

"I usually go to Hairy's," she said, "or the Townhouse. Club Metro before they closed. I'm relatively new to the scene."

"The Townhouse isn't a Were bar," Bjorn noted.

"I'm not exactly what you'd think of as Were," she said with humor in her eyes. "Consider me a fellow traveler."

Bjorn jerked his head to indicate the people still at the tables. In the dining room below, werewolves and werecats and a few other creatures were taking tables, basking in moonglow slanting in through the window-wall. There was the faint click-and-scratch of claws, an occasional screech or growl, and purrs and yips of happiness as friends greeted each other.

"You're still the same person that came in the door," Bjorn noted.

She sipped her drink. "You can never step twice into the same river, my friend. You of all people should know that 'same' is a relative word."

Bjorn shook his head in puzzlement, and reached under the bar for a bowl of raspberries. "The harvest is in," he said as he scooped a pawfull into his mouth. "Care for some berries?"

She took one, popped it in her mouth, savored it. A drop of juice glistened on her lower lip. "One thing about an omnivore," she said, smiling. "You can satisfy your primal hungers without killing something."

Bjorn took another pawfull, then bit into a honeycomb. "Amen!" he growled. "I see you *do* know a few things." And he shambled down the bar to another customer.

Lena finished her bouillon, then caught Bjorn's eye. "Any chance of getting a bowl of those berries? With cream?"

He brought them. She paid, and moved over to a table with a better view of the dining-room below. Erica had gone into the women's changing room. She hadn't come out, so she was probably downstairs. Erica had looked to weigh about one-forty; Lena watched the Weres below, making quick estimates of weight.

Coming up the stairs was one of the most beautiful Weres Lena had ever seen – a mist-grey Angora rabbit, carrying a salad plate. She came over to Lena's table, and gestured to a chair.

"Mind if I join you? I'm uncomfortable in a dining room full of werewolves. They eat too vigorously."

"My name's Lena. Sit and be welcome, but don't let the berries fool you: I'm an omnivore myself." Lena added, "No offense, but a were-*rabbit?* I didn't know there were any of you."

"Rabbits bite, if you startle them. Just my luck to have a pet with the virus. I've half a mind to bite her back and see how she likes being one of the Wee Folk three nights a month. But that'd cause more trouble than it's worth."

She picked up a carrot, held it, waggled her brows. "Ehhh, *crunch* what's up, doc? Call me Bugs. It reminds the wolves I'm not a safe rabbit to chase."

Lena looked at Bugs' front teeth, and agreed. They giggled. Bugs fed Lena a cherry tomato; Lena fed Bugs some raspberries. They bought a pitcher of V-8 juice, and sat happily talking of shoes and ships and sealing-wax, of cabbages and kings; and what the Weres do late at night, and other curious things.

The evening passed pleasantly. Quite a few of the regulars came casually by to look at the newcomer, which suited Lena – she could look them over herself. Two of Bugs' friends sat with them a while – Mao, a were-Siamese, and Judy, a were-husky. Bugs and Mao were both about one-forty. Judy weighed at least two hundred, and definitely wasn't a candidate for *this* investigation.

Karaoke started, with Judy singing "Werewolves of London". Mao and two other werecats harmonized on a few pieces from "Cats". And Lena was in full retreat when a were-poodle started in on "How Much is that Doggie in the Window?" accompanied by yelps from the audience.

As she drove home, the moon rode high; to the right, the river glistened. The howls of moonstruck Weres came faintly from below. Lena thought of the evening. There'd been dozens of Weres, almost as many normals. Erica hadn't been seen – as Erica - after sunset. If she hadn't left unseen for the wildlands below, Bugs and Mao seemed the best candidates for Erica's other life.

She needed more information.

It was just short of midnight, and Paul had said she could call until then. She pulled into an overlook, took out her cell phone. She dialed.

Second Night of the Moon

At sundown, Lena pulled into the Outlook's lot. She walked to the entrance in the fading light. Inside she stood a moment, searching the room, then headed towards a table where a tanned man in white shirt and Dockers was waving.

Paul saw a tall woman at the door, with sandy hair in a short pageboy, and freckles. She wore a gold linen sleeveless blouse with umber slacks and canvas flats. She looked very much like Len: almost certainly, his sister Lena. He waved.

She moved towards him, growing more beautiful with each step. A slight stumble spoiled the magic, but Paul only found that, too, charming. She reached the table, held out her hand. "Paul Johnson?" she said in a rich contralto, the voice he'd heard on the phone last night.

"And you must be Lena Scott. You *do* look like your brother, though you're certainly the more elegant dresser." He hadn't taken his eyes off her for a second.

"I seem to have arrived just at the witching hour," she said as she sat. "Bjorn changed while I was crossing the room." They looked towards the bar, and a bear stood where a man had been moments ago.

"This is good timing. The dining room is just opening; let's get a table," she continued. "That'll give us a better view of the patrons."

As they went down the stairs, she thought, *and it'll give you a bit of an education.* Last night Paul had shown less familiarity with Weres and with Erica than she'd expected. He hadn't even known if she kept a pet. And hadn't known why the question was important. "Have you eaten at a Were bar before?"

"I've eaten here a few times," Paul replied. "Never at the full moon, though."

Lena chose a table for two where she could see Bjorn at the bar, and he could see her. "This table," she said as she sat. Paul sat across from her.

The room was mostly empty. There was a woman in a green-and-gold running suit at a table on the patio, chatting amiably with a skunk. Moonlight and dim fixtures lit the room, and the windows to the south looked past trees to the river. Lights moved along the highway on the far side. Now the doors from the changing rooms were opening, and Weres began to spill down the stairs into the dining room.

The room overfilled, as if dozens of hyperactive teenagers had entered – teens wearing fur suits, armed with fangs and claws. Rough-housing on the men's side turned into a scuffle, two werewolves rolling over and over on the floor, snapping at each other. Again, there were yelps and purrs of welcome; and the scuffling wolves untangled themselves before they reached the center of the room.

"I don't think they want Bjorn to see them tussling," Lena said. "It's his bar, and his tables they might knock over. Even a werewolf would rather not be disciplined by a were-bear."

A waiter was at their table – a human. *Yes,* Lena thought, *hands have their place.* She glanced quickly at the menu. "I'll have the buffaloburger, and a glass of spicy V-8 with a celery stick."

"Steak tartare," Paul said, "and a stein of Beck's Dark."

"I'm sorry, sir. We don't serve alcohol during the full moon." The waiter didn't look particularly sorry. "Would you care for a non-alcoholic beer?"

Paul shook his head. "I'll have coffee."

The waiter left. Lena raised an eyebrow. "Alcohol isn't safe at a Were bar during the full moon. Poor impulse control, this time of the month? Bad idea." She folded her arms before her on the table. "Did you see Erica here?"

Paul leaned towards her. "Yes, but I don't think she saw me. She went up into the changing room about the same time as everybody else."

Over Paul's shoulder, Lena could see Bugs and Judy talking with the skunk and the woman in green. Bugs looked up at the same time, and saw Lena. She started to smile, then saw Paul and turned away. Judy hurried after her.

"If you saw her going into the changing room, she's almost certainly a Were," Lena said. "That's not a safe time and place for normal humans."

"Yes, but she said 'werewolf'. I want to be sure."

"Silly," Lena said as she shook her head. Amber earrings flashed in the moonlight. "There's probably not a single true werewolf here. You're dreaming the impossible dream."

"If werewolves are so rare, who's in this room with us?"

"Were-dogs, mostly. Where are you going to find a wolf to bite you? Dogs and cats, easy. Rabbits, even. And there's a skunk over there. You wouldn't want to meet a genuine werewolf. Dogs get along with people much better than wolves do. They like to be called 'werewolf'. But that doesn't make it so."

Paul looked as if Lena had taken away his toy.

Waiters began arriving with food: joints and chops and steaks and turkey-legs, mostly raw, and sushi. One werewolf, dancing with impatience, snatched his steak before the waiter had set down the plate, began tearing at it. There were growls and snarls and gulping sounds, and Weres glancing sidelong at each other. The copper smell of blood filled the air.

"Where's our food?" Paul said after a while. "We ordered first."

"*Our* food has to be prepared," Lena said. "*Their* food only had to be warmed to blood heat." Paul looked stricken. "And you don't want a Were getting impatient for dinner."

"Oh dear," Paul said. The waiter placed steak tartare before him. He looked at it cautiously.

"It won't bite you," Lena said. "You're supposed to bite it." She took a healthy chunk from her burger, and washed it down with V-8. She wiped red from the corner of her mouth. There were crunching sounds from the next table.

Paul gulped, stood, and headed for the exit. Lena threw a fifty on the table, and followed. She caught Bjorn's eye as she passed the bar, pointed to her table. "We'll settle the details later!"

Paul was in the parking lot, standing by a low-rider Cruiser. Lena hurried up to him, saw the distress on his face, saw the reason the car was riding so low. Its tires were shredded.

She caught his arm. "Tooth-marks. Bet those tires tasted awful, too. Somebody must be *angry*. And only *your* car is damaged. This is not a good place to be." She began pulling him back towards the Outlook.

Bjorn met them at the door. "Can't take it inside, don't like it outside?" Paul glared. Lena stood between them. "Bjorn, somebody chewed Paul's tires. It's not safe for him out here. We need your protection."

"Like hell we do," Paul growled. He spun on his foot and began walking away.

"He's a damn fool," Bjorn said. "Anybody who doesn't know when to be scared shouldn't hang around Were bars."

"He's the damn fool that's paying me," Lena said. "I'd better talk some sense into him." She ran after Paul.

"Hold up," she cried. "We're getting further from my car every minute." But he continued towards the main highway. Behind her there was a rustle in the bushes, and a soft growl.

"Freeze, Paul! Don't do anything that makes you look like prey. There's a werewolf in the bushes."

A flash of motion, a gleam of white teeth, and Judy was bounding past Lena towards Paul. Lena leaned, reached, grabbed Judy by the hindleg; swooped her up into a whirl, spun three times, picking up speed and motion as she danced across the lot, then threw her in the air down the bluff. Lena ran towards Paul.

"Now run! Fast!"

There was a ruined old house nearby, with the fieldstone fireplace and chimney still standing. Paul headed for the chimney, began to climb. Lena raced after him, climbed behind him. They reached the top at the same instant. It was barely large enough for both of them.

"I didn't know you were a rock-climber," Paul said.

"I got the urge to try about half a minute ago."

Judy came loping up the road, began clumsily trying to climb the chimney towards them. She was growling low in her throat.

Lena took a small canister from her purse. She showed it to the werewolf. "Pepper spray," she said. "Your nose is a hundred times more sensitive than mine. It'd be embarrassing, getting done in by a vegetable extract."

Her eyes on the spray, tail quivering furiously, Judy began to back down. In the distance, Lena saw Bjorn heading towards them. The moon shone serenely; a nighthawk made its breathy, whistling sound. Judy bounded into the brush, disappeared in shadows.

They made their way down the chimney, and Bjorn escorted them back to Lena's car. "I'll send a wrecker for my car," Paul said to Bjorn as they left. "Tomorrow, in daylight."

Lena drove with a lead foot until they were several miles from the Outlook, then slowed. "We're in trouble with the Weres," she said. "I hope it's a hissy-fit instead of something more permanent."

"What did we do?"

"You ordered raw meat, then didn't eat it. That says 'wannabe' to a lot of Weres. And I should have realized Erica – or her friends – might think you were two-timing her if they saw us together. Or, just maybe, they realized you were having her investigated."

Lena gripped the steering wheel, looked at Paul from below lowered brows. "Tonight, and tomorrow night, you stay locked up at home. I'm going back to mend fences."

Third Night of the Moon

Lena wore running shoes, sweats, and no jewelry. It was half an hour to sunset. On the third night of the moon, that would give her an hour and a half to talk before everybody went Were. And freedom of movement, just in case.

With the sun still in the sky, The Outlook was quiet. Bjorn was behind the bar preparing for the night, and serving the occasional early-comers. Lena chose a quiet spot, sat down, and waited.

Bjorn came over. "You put down a fifty, but the tab only came to thirty-four."

"Keep the rest," Lena said. "We gave you enough trouble last night."

"Maybe, but I should apologize too. I didn't realize somebody'd chewed up your boyfriend's tires. I don't run that kind of bar."

"He's not my boyfriend. He's a business associate. But that's something I should talk with Bugs about, I think. Is she angry? And what about Judy?"

"Don't worry about Judy. She was talking half the night about that throw you handed her. 'Almost as good as the Slingshot at the State Fair', she said."

"It's amazing what a girl will do under the moon, in the passion of the moment." Lena smiled in the dimness.

"You'll have to explain that to me some time, if you get to be a regular here." Bjorn paused and sniffed the air, then looked thoughtful. "I might have a few suspicions, though."

"And you might be right," Lena said as she marked a score in the air with her forefinger. "And Bugs might have a few other suspicions, and she might be wrong. Think it'll be okay for me to stay and talk with her, if she comes in?"

"I don't see any problems. Not if you have a good line of talk, anyway."

"I intend to speak softly, and carry a big bowl of raspberries. Can I get a bowl of raspberries and cream, say half an hour before moonrise? And some carrots?"

"Sure."

When Erica came into the bar, Lena was at the same table she'd met Bugs at. Almost everybody had been stopping by to say hello to the woman who'd thrown Judy, and Lena had been smiling and greeting them all; when Erica passed, Lena did exactly the same to her.

By moonrise, Lena was no longer a newcomer to the Outlook.

Five minutes later, Bugs joined her. She flipped her paw at the carrots. "Looks like an invitation to talk," she said.

"We need to. There was a rather spectacular misunderstanding last night, and you and I seem to have been near the center of it."

"*Moi?*" Bugs said.

"Paul's tires looked like the Giant Rat of Sumatra was chewing on them. That, or somebody else with gnawing teeth."

"The two-timing rat seemed to *own* the car, not gnaw the tires."

"Actually, Paul's sin wasn't two-timing, but hiring an investigator. To find out if one Erica Schmidt is really a werewolf as advertised. I'm the investigator."

Bugs whopped herself upside the head. "Fleas are enough of a worry this time of the month, now I've got investigators too?"

"He hired me knowing I was discreet," Lena said. "And he obviously doesn't know what he's getting into. So I'll tell him only that Erica is indeed Were, and that the denizens of the Outlook are werewolves by common nomenclature - but none are true werewolves. Erica, and Paul, can take it from there."

Bugs lifted a carrot. "Ehhhhh, *crunch* - he's in for an interesting time...."

"It will probably give him a few grey hares," Lena agreed.

Judy came over to join them. "Looks like you two have made up. I'm sorry I made such a fuss last night. Bugs is a *very* good friend, and I didn't like seeing her hurt. But you handed me quite a surprise!"

"Poor impulse control," they chorused in unison.

They talked for a while longer, then Lena noted that it was time for her to be off. "Reports to give, checks to collect, things like that. Maybe teach Werewolf Etiquette 101 to Paul. I'll be seeing you both, later." She rose, and left.

In half an hour, she was at Paul's door. He let her in, motioned her to a chair. The room was unpretentious and comfortable, with photos of trails and rock formations. A sturdy end table sat next to the chair, and a good reading light.

"I smoothed things over," she began. "Erica thought you were two-timing her. That wolf last night was one of her friends, angry on her behalf.

"Erica *is* Were. But she said 'werewolf' because that's the generic. She's not a wolf, and would rather know you better before she has you meet her other half. You'd be safe, with her."

Paul wrote a check for fees and expenses, then sighed. "I didn't get my Beck's Dark last night. I think I'll have one now."

"I'll take a Bloody Mary, if you have the makings." Why *not* have a drink? It had been a tense evening.

Going into the kitchen Paul moved well, with coordination and control and a spring in his step. Lena was noticing he was a very attractive man. The refrigerator door opened and closed. She heard liquids being poured and stirred. Paul returned with a stein of dark beer, and a Bloody Mary in a tall glass. He'd even remembered the celery stick. Lena took the glass with a smile.

"You didn't seem as familiar with a Were bar as I'd expect from somebody who likes werewolves," she said after her first drink.

He dimpled, and sipped his beer. "I hardly thought of werewolves until two months ago when I started dating Erica. But when I asked her to a concert a month ago – last full moon – she said all her full moons were taken, and told me why."

"A month is awfully fast to get *that* interested in Weres."

"I get enthusiastic. It fits nicely alongside a werewolf's impulsiveness." Paul shrugged.

Lena drank, then nibbled her celery. "So why did you decide she might not be Were? Enough to pay to find out?"

"Well, I wanted to go out with her during the moon. And she was evasive. I began to wonder."

"Not only enthusiastic, but impatient?"

Lena was beginning to feel warm, warmer than the alcohol, or even the Tabasco, in her drink could explain. She looked at Paul.

They'd shared danger the night before – and he'd been a damnfool to get into it, but he'd handled himself well when it counted. She remembered their eyes meeting at the top of the chimney.

Their eyes met. They were silent.

Their bodies met halfway between their chairs, and Lena didn't have the slightest idea who'd made the first move. *Darn that poor impulse control!* They kissed, long and firmly. His left hand cradled her head; she kneaded the muscles in his back. She paused for a breath, then dove back in. And four urgent hands began to misbehave.

He lifted her up, and carried her into the bedroom.

The Morning After

Paul woke slowly, languidly, to the sun glowing through the curtains. He was nude; and beside him, Lena slept on. He studied her face, thought of the night just past. Tenderly, his hand reached out to brush her cheek.

Stubble.

Green eyes opened sleepily at his touch, looked at him, smiled apologetically. "I was bitten by a woman," she said in a tenor voice.

Paul's mind whirled as his world took a new shape. "You're *Len!*" he said, backing away.

"Only since moonset," Len said with a wry grin. "For which you should be thankful. Imagine how complicated it would have been if I'd changed at midnight, like Cinderella."

"But dammit …" Paul said, "… you were Lena *before* all the other Weres changed!"

"Oh, *I* change at moonrise and moonset," Len said. "But nobody bit my clothes. Don't *you* dress ahead of time for whatever *you* expect to be doing? And you said it yourself about werewolves –" Len's body-language and posture shifted. His voice went contralto. It was as if Lena were back.

"You can see a bit of wolf in them all month long."

CYCLES OF VIOLENCE

Normally, the waxing moon was a good time to own a were bar. It was only the middle of the afternoon, but there were a dozen customers at the booths and tables already, clustered in small groups, chattering and cheerful, with an air of anticipation about them. They were eating, drinking, spending money, and behaving well – much less rowdy than they'd be come the full moon.

And here Len's friend Bjorn was, standing behind the bar, acting as if he were waiting for the other shoe to drop. That wasn't like Bjorn at *all*.

Finally Bjorn sighed, mixed a Bloody Mary, and filled a tankard of mead for himself. He went to a booth where he could watch both the bar and the entrance, motioned Len over, and handed the blood-red drink to him. Bjorn sat for a while, took a sip of mead, and leaned back with a distant look in his eyes. He spoke.

"About a hundred fifty years ago, my family had a run-in with Wendigo. My great-great-grandfather Ulfbjorn had come from Norway to Minnesota for the opportunity. There was land to be had, and work cutting down trees, and all kinds of fur-animals. It was good bear territory. Lots of Norwegians were coming here, and Swedes, and even a few Finns.

"We'd brought our own heritage with us, our legends and tales and bloodlines. Were-bears are different, you know. For most of us it's in the blood when we're born. We don't need to be bitten by

129

something, like the werewolves and the others. And we aren't ruled by the Moon.

"Ulfbjorn needed a stake before he tried anything ambitious, so he signed up with Paul Bunyan to do some lumbering. Paul was quite a legend already, even at his young age. He could beat great-great at arm-wrestling, though family stories say the odds were more even when it was full-body wrestling. Bears are great wrestlers, after all."

Len Scott — about half Bjorn's size and nowhere as hairy — sipped his drink. "Does this story include Babe the Blue Ox? I'm already starting to notice the bull."

"No, Babe never got into the story. Great worker, that ox, but he headed straight for the barn when the day's lumbering was over. And this happened after dark.

"Paul had hired some Indians to hunt for him. He had a hungry crew, and it took a lot to feed them; but deer and moose were abundant, and the local people were better at finding them than Paul's folk.

"Now, one of the Indians looked different, and didn't hang around with the others. Quite a loner. He'd come from far away, but didn't like to talk about it. And he never seemed to be around during the full moon.

"Great-great grandfather could see the signs, so he cultivated the man. His name was Yellow Horse. They'd sit together of an evening, smoking their pipes and talking. Yellow Horse began to warm up to great-great; and it soon became plain they shared something.

"Ulfbjorn was a were-bear, of course. And Yellow Horse was a werewolf, though his people called them 'skinwalkers'. They'd driven him out. Most settled people don't approve of werewolves. And Yellow Horse was a *real* werewolf, not the sort of 'wolf' we get today."

"Ah-HEM!" Len cleared his throat.

"Oh, no offense intended to you, or your friends, or the customers at my club. But the world was more stark in the old days, before we started having all these newfangled Weres showing up.

And I guess the new Weres are a good thing, because there's less bloodshed, but these old family stories make me nostalgic.

"Where was I? Oh, yes. Ulfbjorn and Yellow Horse got to be close friends. They decided to go adventuring together when the full moon came. They set off early in the afternoon, so they would be well away from camp before moonrise, and headed for a patch of forest the Indians avoided. 'Bad medicine,' the locals said.

"The sun was almost down, and it had gotten pretty dark in the trees. Great-great was eating some blueberries he had found, while Yellow Horse was drinking from a stream a way off. They saw a pale form in the forest. It must have been eight feet tall, but it vanished almost before they saw it. No matter how hard they looked, they couldn't find it.

"And then it came out from behind a tree, and grabbed Yellow Horse. 'I'm Wendigo,' it said, 'and I'm hungry. Somebody here is going to get eaten.'

"Just then the sun must have slipped below the horizon, because Yellow Horse changed. He looked up at Wendigo, and said 'Best two out of three?'

"Wendigo had a bright star in its forehead, and it was dressed in white robes. Great-great grandfather said it looked like a *ljosalf*, a bright-elf. It was very surprised, because in all the time it had been eating Indians, none of them had ever turned into wolves before.

"They started in fighting. First it went hard on Yellow Horse, because Wendigo had a good grip; but he managed to get Wendigo's arm in his jaws, and began chewing his way up. Wendigo was dancing around, shaking its arm and trying to get the wolf off and banging Yellow Horse into trees. Great-great-grandfather was sitting back and watching the ruckus, laughing his head off.

"It must have been the laughter that did it. Soon Yellow Horse and Wendigo stopped fighting and were both staring at Ulfbjorn, and it wasn't necessarily a friendly stare. 'What's so funny?' they both asked.

"'*Something I disagreed with ate me!*'" Ulfbjorn said, which was nothing less than the truth. Both Yellow Horse and Wendigo had chewed off chunks of each other in the fuss. Ulfbjorn broke out into fresh gales of laughter, and pretty soon they all were rolling around on the ground laughing. There had been no real harm done in the fight, except to the trees, because both Wendigo and werewolves heal fast and well."

As Bjorn was talking, a low growling had started outside, gradually getting louder and closer. It resolved into the sound of many motorcycles. They came into the parking lot, throttled up and down several times, and stopped in a chorus of mechanical coughing.

Bjorn put his hand on Len's arm, and looked at the others in the bar. "Let me handle this."

A large man came in the door, every bit as large as Bjorn. He had wild hair, topped by a greasy bandanna. His torso was bare except for a black leather vest, windburned, covered with curly black hair. Several scars crossed it. His arms were the same, with burn-marks and disturbing tattoos. His hands were massive, the knuckles badly abused, with motor-grease and grime under ragged nails. Behind him were at least a dozen smaller variations on the same theme.

"We're the Wendigos," he said. "We were in the neighborhood, so we thought we'd drop in to play with a few werewolves." His voice did not suggest he had softball in mind.

Bjorn smiled and shook his head. "You've come at the wrong time for that. Drop by in a week, when it's the full moon, and we'll have werewolves for you."

"We're an impatient bunch," the cyclist said. "We'll make do by playing with their friends, and their dainty little clubhouse." His eyes moved about the room, taking in the dozen or so people in the booths or at the bar or tables. His followers started spreading out through the room. The customers watched them come, and didn't seem nearly as unsettled as the cyclists might have wished.

"I'm going to insist you play nicely," Bjorn said. "It's the rule here."

"Wendigos don't play by the rules."

Bjorn lost his smile as he moved closer to the self-styled Wendigo.

"I know Wendigo, my friend, and you are no Wendigo. For one thing, Wendigo is at least eight feet tall, and I wouldn't rate you at better than six-five.

"Also, there is only the one Wendigo; there must be at least a dozen of you.

"Finally, if I pulled the arms and legs off Wendigo and fed them to the wolves, Wendigo would be ready to go another round with me the next day. I don't think you could measure up to that.

"Mind you," Bjorn said with a very different smile, one that showed his teeth, "I won't have any wolves for a week or so. But I do have a refrigerator to keep the arms and legs in, for them. Want to make the experiment? I'll even give you the extra week to get back in shape for the fight." Bjorn reached out and took one shoulder of the Wendigo claimant in each of his own massive hands. They locked eyes. The customers – and the other cyclists – watched.

There was a cold aura of sullen menace about the cyclist, but it was overshadowed by Bjorn's hot aura of barely-restrained bloodlust. The air shimmered about them. The cyclist felt claws digging into his shoulders. The rank, wild scent of Bear filled the air.

The cyclist's face went pale, and another scent joined the Bear.

Bjorn sadly let go, and patted the cyclist gently on the shoulder. "No," he said, "I guess you *don't* want to play after all. You'd probably much rather go home and change your pants."

Silently, shamefacedly, the giant cyclist dropped his head. He looked much smaller than he had when he'd come in. He waddled to the door, and out; and his followers – followed. Bjorn stood alone in the center of the floor.

He went over to the booth he'd been sharing with Len, picked up his tankard of mead, and downed it in one gulp. He went behind the bar, filled it, and emptied it again. Then he filled it yet again, and went over to sit with his friend. He blew out a great gust of air, and slumped. "That was very close," he said.

"You didn't *look* worried," Len said.

"He was one *mean* fellow," Bjorn said. "I had to push myself almost to the edge of berserk to scare him off. If he hadn't backed down, I might have gone over and turned bear.

"The law makes such a fuss these days when you rip somebody to shreds. Pity — folk used to figure anybody foolish enough to challenge a berserk deserved what he got.

"Stop and think. I could have taken him easily. But he had a dozen friends, and I never could have caught them all, let alone eaten them. And what would I do about the motorcycles? One of those fellows would have gone yelling to the police, and there we'd be with blood and bones and scraps of clothing on the floor, and motorcycles in our parking lot. That wouldn't be good. I'd have to take off for the Northwoods, and the rest of you would lose the club."

"I wasn't thinking that far ahead," Len admitted. They both sat in silence as they finished their drinks, and so did all the other customers.

Bjorn went behind the bar. "This one's on the house!" he shouted, and everybody came to refill their steins and glasses. They'd resumed their cheerful talk, but now their eyes and gestures pointed towards Bjorn often as not. They seemed impressed and satisfied.

Len sat on a stool, leaned on the bar. "You never did finish your story," he said. "And it doesn't seem a coincidence for you to be talking about Wendigo when those other 'wendigos' appeared."

Bjorn smiled. "There's not much more to the story. Ulfbjorn and Yellow Horse and Wendigo went off and killed a deer, and had a good meal together and a good talk. But they split up well before dawn. When Yellow Horse turned back into a man at sunrise, he didn't want to be anywhere near Wendigo. Could you blame him?

"Since then, we've kept in touch. Even when you're the meanest fellow in the Valley of the Shadow of Death, it's a good idea to keep track of the fellows in the other valleys. If you step on their toes, you don't want it to be an accident or a surprise.

"Now would you be astonished to find a werewolf — one of the old-fashioned, bloodthirsty kind — in a motorcycle gang? Not that they know he's a werewolf.

"Apparently there's been a leadership struggle among the motorcyclists. Yellow Horse's great-great-great grandson, Red Dog, found out that Crank, our recently-departed playmate, was planning this visit to build his reputation as a dangerous man. That could firm up Crank's position as leader.

"Red Dog gave me a call. For a wild one like him, friends are hard to come by. He didn't want to lose any, and figured giving me time to think might help. I've been thinking it over ever since; excuse me if I've seemed distracted.

"Of course with Crank this thoroughly embarrassed, Red Dog might take over the Wendigos. He'd like that. It's the way in-group politics goes, and probably another reason he called me. I hope he wasn't behind this all, just to get in charge. If I found out he was, I'd have to admonish him."

They sat, and drank their respective drinks, and contemplated the sins of politicians, no matter *what* their momentary species or affiliation. Werewolves were good, werewolves were fine, but they didn't want any politicians coming around the club. It would knock down the tone.